THE BAYOU BULLETIN

Marie Delacroix Accused In Client's Death

Marie Delacroix, 29, second oldest daughter of federal judge Justin Delacroix, has been accused in the mysterious death of her client, David Markum, on December 5.

Markum, a long-time patron of Delacroix's aromatherapy shop, Heaven Scent, had been receiving a cure at the time of his sudden demise. Paramedics called to the scene initially attributed the death to a heart attack, but Dr. Carl Lee Shivley, Chief Coroner at Lakeview Community Hospital,

says a toxicology screen run by Deputy Coroner Dr. Lucas Henderson turned up some inconsistencies.

"Something about the whole thing just didn't set right with me," said Shivley, contacted in his office.

A search of Marie Delacroix's shop turned up a suspicious substance in the oil used on Markum. She is currently being arraigned on a charge of manslaughter.

Approached by this reporter, Dr. Lucas Henderson had only one comment. "She killed David Markum and now we can prove it."

If you purchased this book without a cover you should be aware that this book is stolen property. It was reported as "unsold and destroyed" to the publisher, and neither the author nor the publisher has received any payment for this "stripped book."

Rhonda Harding Pollero is acknowledged
as the author of this work.

In loving memory of my aunt, Helen Hale DeSimone
(1928-1996), a woman who truly knew how to enjoy life.

ISBN 0-373-82564-1

IN THE BRIDE'S DEFENSE

Copyright © 1997 by Harlequin Books S.A.

All rights reserved. Except for use in any review, the reproduction or utilization of this work in whole or in part in any form by any electronic, mechanical or other means, now known or hereafter invented, including xerography, photocopying and recording, or in any information storage or retrieval system, is forbidden without the written permission of the publisher, Harlequin Enterprises Limited, 225 Duncan Mill Road, Don Mills, Ontario, Canada M3B 3K9.

All characters in this book have no existence outside the imagination of the author and have no relation whatsoever to anyone bearing the same name or names. They are not even distantly inspired by any individual known or unknown to the author, and all incidents are pure invention.

This edition published by arrangement with Harlequin Books S.A.

® and TM are trademarks of the publisher. Trademarks indicated with ® are registered in the United States Patent and Trademark Office, the Canadian Trade Marks Office and in other countries.

Printed in U.S.A.

DELTA JUSTICE

In the Bride's Defense

Kelsey Roberts

Harlequin Books

TORONTO • NEW YORK • LONDON
AMSTERDAM • PARIS • SYDNEY • HAMBURG
STOCKHOLM • ATHENS • TOKYO • MILAN
MADRID • WARSAW • BUDAPEST • AUCKLAND

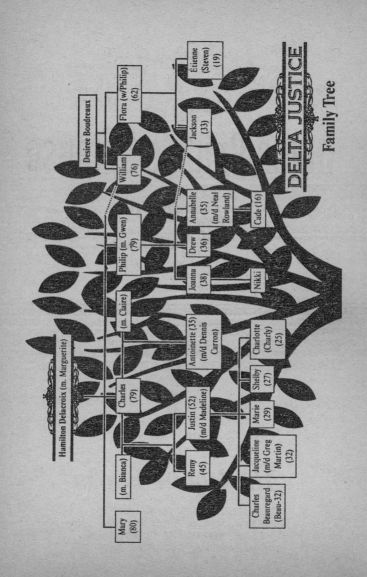

Hamilton Delacroix (m. Marguerite)

Desiree Boudreaux

Mary (80)

(m. Bianca)

Charles (79)

(m. Claire)

William (76)

Flora (w/Philip) (62)

Philip (m. Gwen) (79)

Remy (45)

Justin (52) (m/d Madeline)

Antoinette (35) (m/d Dennis Carron)

Joanna (38)

Drew (36)

Annabelle (35) (m/d Neal Rowland)

Jackson (33)

Etienne (Steven) (19)

Charles Beauregard (Beau–32)

Jacqueline (m/d Greg Martin) (32)

Marie (29)

Shelby (27)

Charlotte (Charly) (25)

Nikki

Cade (16)

DELTA JUSTICE
Family Tree

CAST OF CHARACTERS

Marie Delacroix—This Delacroix woman had an unconventional way of living life. Had she ended David's just as unconventionally?

Lucas Henderson—The deputy coroner and forensic pathologist assigned to the Markum case. Is falling in love with the chief suspect a conflict of interest?

Carl Lee Shivley—The coroner at Lakeview Community Hospital—and Lucas's boss. Carl is out for Delacroix blood…but why?

David Markum—Marie's client and the man she's accused of killing. Were they more than friends?

Ken Rogers—another one of Marie's clients.

Graham Nash—David Markum's business partner. He had the most to gain from David's death.

Desiree Boudreaux—Had Marie's good friend put a little something extra in the herbal remedies she concocted?

Justin Delacroix—Marie's father, and former senior partner at Delacroix and Associates. The judge will do anything—anything—to protect his little girl.

Dear Reader,

There are very few places as romantic and mysterious as the bayous of Louisiana. The blend of cultures, religions and traditions was a sheer joy to explore. My research included learning about voodoo, Wicca, incense, oils, candles, brews and the clearing and enhancing of energy in the home. My husband probably would have been happier if I had studied the idea of clearing and cleaning my house with as much interest.

I had an image of Marie Delacroix from the very start of the project. Incorporating her rather unique interests into a believable romance was challenging but fun. Marie is a medical school dropout who has turned to nontraditional healing with an emphasis on aromatherapy. Unfortunately, circumstances require her to work closely with the very traditional Lucas Henderson, M.D. Marie not only rejects most of what Lucas holds as gospel, she also rejects him. A murder, an overzealous assistant district attorney, a voodoo priestess and some odd coincidences force these opposites together, but for how long?

I'm very pleased to have been asked to tell you Marie and Lucas's story as part of Harlequin's DELTA JUSTICE series, and I hope you'll continue to follow the adventures of the Delacroix clan in the coming months.

Enjoy!

Warmest regards,

Kelsey Roberts

PROLOGUE

"Now, DAVID," Marie intoned soothingly as she lit first a white candle, then a purple one, "lie back and close your eyes...relax."

"I'd love to," David answered, lowering his head to the pillow. "Lately I've been having trouble sleeping."

Marie frowned as she mixed juniper, lotus bouquet and eucalyptus into the base oil she had blended specifically for him. The rushing sounds of a gentle wind were carried into the treatment room by small speakers hidden behind the heavy fabric wall coverings. "I'm sensing a great deal of tension in you today," she commented as she worked on the potion.

"Things at the retreat are a little hectic," he admitted.

"You and your profession are in an extreme state of discord. But I'm sensing something more here."

He lifted his head and stared at her. "You're very perceptive, Marie. You should have continued on in medical school."

"You sound like my father," she said with a sigh, then looked him straight in the eye. "We've been friends a long time, David. What is it that's really bothering you?"

David shook his head before returning to a prone

position. "I'll work it out. Your oils and incantations are making the pain in my shoulder better."

Marie smiled. "I'm sure once you deal with your problems, you'll get over this insomnia. Now, let's begin."

She began to rub the fragrant oil into the arthritic shoulder. The scent was strong, meant to last until his next visit. Closing her eyes, she mentally recited an incantation to rid this man of his pain. "Have you been experiencing any other pain?"

"I think the arthritis is spreading. Some of my other joints are beginning to ache."

"Then I'll mix an extra dosage and we'll nip this in the bud before the pain becomes intolerable."

The massage lasted a full half hour, leaving David somewhat more relaxed by the time she had finished. "While you let the oil penetrate, I'll go into the front of the shop and fix you an amulet and some tea."

"I can't counsel couples with garlic hanging around my neck," he said hesitantly.

"No garlic," she assured him, keeping her voice soft so she wouldn't disturb the healing aura. "You'll need to wear a gold chain with a turquoise pendant. We have to stop the spread of the arthritis."

"I'll look a little silly running around New Orleans dressed like an Indian chief."

"Wear it inside your shirt," she instructed. "Do you have an old wedding band? Preferably one that has been in your family for a few generations?"

"Sorry, no family heirlooms."

"That's okay," she said. "You'll have to buy a new one from a jeweler. A new one doesn't work as quickly, but if it's solid gold, that should speed things along.''

"Okay," he said, and started to rise.

"Rest for a few minutes. You look tired and you need to calm down so your hands stop shaking. Have you been drinking coffee instead of tea?''

His only answer was a guilty look.

"When you put the amulet on, say, Pain to stone, save me.''

"If you insist," he answered warily.

"I'll mix up some herbal teas while you relax and concentrate on ridding your body of pain and negative energy. When you go home, stay off the coffee, drink the tea, and we'll reassess the pain at your next appointment.''

"You sound like a doctor, Marie.''

"I'm an aromatherapist," she corrected him automatically. The descendant of three generations of lawyers, she was acutely aware of her legal responsibilities regarding disclaimers. "I shudder to think of myself trapped in the confines of traditional medicine. This way I can offer people an alternative, and I didn't have to wade through eight years of biology to do it. Speaking of helping people, did that friend of yours get rid of his headaches?''

"What friend?" he asked.

Marie shrugged. "Rogers, I think his name is. He's been something of a regular. He said you suggested he come in for a powder to help his migraines, and now he's hooked.''

"I tell a lot of people about you. That was our deal.''

"I really appreciate that, David. Especially since I

haven't exactly held up my end of our deal. I hope you understand that I wasn't comfortable letting people think we're a couple.'' Marie smiled and patted his hand. "I wouldn't mind a few more customers like him," she said, and turned to leave.

As she passed through the curtain of crystal beads that separated the treatment area from the front of the small shop where she sold oils, candles, incense and every other homeopathic remedy known, Marie shivered unexpectedly and a sudden and fierce chill danced along her spine.

"Maybe Desiree is doing a reading on me," she whispered as she pushed aside the box containing the Christmas decorations she hoped to put up today. Desiree's healing powers were well-known and respected by all who had experienced her ministrations firsthand. Marie considered herself lucky to have had Desiree as her teacher. Though she wasn't blessed with the older woman's special sight, Marie had learned the medicinal use of herbs and oils from a true master. And that master watched over her from her remote cabin in the swamp. Desiree made it her business to forewarn Marie of any great changes upcoming in her life.

Her warning from the previous week was still etched in Marie's consciousness. *Great turbulence will bring great serenity.* "Hopefully that means I'm going to make this place a success," Marie mused.

She began preparing the various teas, though she was bothered by David's new complaints. It seemed that each visit brought a new symptom. She made a mental note to discuss it with Desiree. David was a psychiatrist. Perhaps he needed to deal with the stresses of his demanding profession before she could effectively relieve the pain in his joints.

Marie flipped open the antique hunter's watch that had been a gift from her father. "I'll let him rest for a while," she murmured. "He sure looked like he could use a nap."

The small bell above the door chimed, and Marie soon found herself with a half-dozen tourists crammed into her small shop. Though she took her profession as an aromatherapist seriously, Heaven Scent, her retail business, also relied heavily on the financial contributions made by nonbelievers.

"May I help you?"

A woman in her late sixties stepped forward. Marie didn't need a crystal ball to know what the woman was thinking. The amused light in her eyes was an instant giveaway.

"Do you have anything to spark up...''

"You're looking for an intimacy enhancer?" Marie asked politely.

"I just want something that will get Joe Rob away from the TV and into the sack. Got anything like that?"

Keeping her practiced smile in place, Marie reached behind the counter and took out a vial of cardamom oil. "This will bring on a jolt of energy as well as increased sexual desire," she explained.

The woman blushed and her friends cackled. "This isn't illegal, is it?"

"No, but you have to mix it with base oil." Marie retrieved a larger bottle and placed it on the counter. "Blend five to seven drops of the cardamom in an eighth of a cup of the base oil."

"What's in this base oil?"

"It's just jojoba oil," Marie explained.

"Do I put it on his..."

Marie grabbed an instruction pamphlet from next to the register and gave it to the woman. "You put it on yourself."

The woman frowned. "I'm not the one with no get-up-and-go."

"The oil is to inspire your husband to want you," she explained over the howls of the others.

"If it works on Joe Rob, I'll have to borrow some the next time those fellows from the electric company come by," one of the others said. This brought yet another round of hoots.

Marie took the woman's money, reminding herself that she needed the capital. She wasn't yet earning enough from her practice to risk offending the curious.

She checked her watch again and decided it was time to get David and send him back to work.

The dozen or so bracelets she wore jingled as she walked back through the beads. "David?"

Nothing.

"David?" she tried again, touching his shoulder. It felt cool and clammy. "David!" she yelled as she struggled to ease him onto his side.

When she finally succeeded, Marie noticed the faint purplish tinge around his mouth, then looked into his wide, lifeless eyes.

CHAPTER ONE

"WHY WAS MY recommendation ignored?" Lucas demanded, slamming a file onto the center of Dr. Shivley's desk.

"Do you always have to raise your voice, Dr. Henderson?"

"You seem to bring out the worst in me," Lucas muttered as he lowered himself into one of the chairs opposite the antique desk that dominated the spacious office. "Want to tell me what this is all about?" He tapped his index finger on the folder.

Without giving the file more than a cursory glance, Carl Lee Shivley shrugged his compact shoulders beneath the jacket of his white seersucker suit. "I read your report. I just don't happen to agree that a full inquest is warranted." The coroner smiled in dismissal. "I know you have forensic training, Doctor. But it seems to be an open-and-shut case to me."

"Did you see the tox screen?" Lucas pressed. "The mercury levels are—"

"High," Carl Lee agreed. "I don't know how she did it, but I've already contacted the D.A."

Lucas raked his hand through his hair. *She* was Marie Delacroix. He didn't even need to close his eyes to recall her image. Marie had the sort of face a man couldn't forget—even if he'd only seen that face in a news photo. "This is bayou country," he argued. "The high mercury levels could have come from eating contaminated shellfish. Proper procedure is to redo the screen to verify the findings. Then I should take another section from—"

Carl Lee's brown eyes narrowed and his indulgent smile began to fade. "I've made my decision, Doctor. If you continue to argue every case with me, I might just begin to regret my decision to appoint you as one of my deputy coroners."

Blowing out a furious breath, Lucas attempted to stem his rising irritation. Carl Lee had a real knack for making him angry. It was the way he played the country-bumpkin doctor, a facade he worked hard to maintain. Lucas had learned that during his first few weeks at New Orleans' Lakeview Community Hospital. Carl Lee Shivley might dress and act like a good ol' boy, but the man was sharp. Lucas decided his best chance was an appeal to the man's intelligence.

"I know you've studied forensics extensively since your appointment as coroner."

"I try to keep current," Carl Lee agreed, loosening the knot of his tie until it became visible beneath his double chin. "Amazing what we can find out from a speck of blood or a grain of dirt."

"Or a *verified* tox screen," Lucas added.

He shook his head ruefully. "I don't seem to be getting through to you, son. The David Markum case is closed for us. The district attorney's office is ready to go forward."

"We don't know that David was murdered."

"Can you imagine the publicity when we charge a Delacroix with murder? Hell, son, you can't turn around in this state without running into one of them,'' Carl Lee quipped, then laughed at his own joke. "Our job now is to figure out how she did it. I'm going to let you handle that part."

"I don't want to handle a half-assed witch-hunt you and the D.A. are conducting for political reasons," Lucas countered. "Forensics isn't a tool to get your name in the paper. The tox screen was preliminary." He waited until he was sure he had the other man's full attention. "I found substantial amounts of mercury salts in the tissues, but I can't identify the source of the contamination without more tests."

Carl Lee sighed, his rotund body heaving with the effort. "That is exactly what you would expect from mercury salts poisoning."

"True. But I could have gotten the same results from a person who had consumed tainted shellfish over a period of time, even though he might not have had shellfish in his stomach at the time of death. Mercury poisoning is usually a slow process resulting from a history of eating contaminated—"

"Enough," Carl Lee snapped. "David Markum didn't die because he ate crawfish from some polluted swamp."

"We don't know that."

Carl Lee rose and stared hard at Lucas. "You're a smart doctor, so listen up. Markum didn't ingest any shellfish. *Ever.*"

Lucas fought to keep his tone civil. "I don't recall seeing that on the reports."

"Wasn't there," Carl Lee admitted. "But I happen to know it's a fact all the same."

"Who gave you the information?"

"No one."

"You're a psychic, too?" Lucas asked, no longer mindful of being civil.

"I know David Markum never ate shellfish because we were—acquainted. David was allergic to seafood."

Lucas was rendered speechless. He didn't like surprises, and this was a huge one. "David and I were roommates in college. He never said anything about an allergy to me."

"I'm sure two young bucks like you had better things to discuss?" Carl Lee suggested with a meaningful lift of his bushy white eyebrows.

Lucas found his boss's bawdy humor grating, but he kept silent.

"I have turned this matter over to the authorities," Carl Lee went on. "Get together the deceased's belongings and then meet the police officer at Miss Delacroix's shop in the Quarter."

"To do what? And if you're so determined to put a Delacroix behind bars, why don't you go?"

"Because I'm not sure what, if anything, you'll find, and I can't look overzealous before we have a solid case built against her." Carl Lee rubbed his jaw pensively. "They only elected me coroner because nobody else ran for the job. Before I ran for coroner, I was postmaster. Before that, I was the superintendent of the school board. Don't let me down, son. My future in this town will be assured if you get the goods on that girl."

"Is there any medical data to support your accusation that this *woman*—" he paused to emphasize the word ''—has any reason to poison a psychiatrist?''

Carl Lee sighed. ''That's what I'm counting on from you. I need proof that Markum died as a result of transdermal poisoning. You're the best forensic man in the state. I'm just asking you to get me the proof I need.''

''Need or want?'' Lucas demanded through clenched teeth. ''We're supposed to do an independent medical evaluation of cases. Not find ways for you to grandstand your way into politics.''

Carl Lee scratched his head. ''Don't forget who is in charge here, son.''

''Is that a threat?''

''Just a friendly warning,'' Carl Lee said, his smile slipping back into place. ''I want Marie Delacroix, and I expect you to get her for me.''

''WHY ISN'T DR. CARL LEE with you?'' Lieutenant Peltier asked Lucas as they walked through Jackson Square. ''He usually likes to be there when we execute a search warrant, just in case one of the TV people shows up.''

Lucas smiled humorlessly. That sounded just like his boss. Carl Lee Shivley seemed to relish the public part of being a public servant. He just wasn't very well suited for the servant end of it. He also had no idea that Lucas had arranged to expand the investigation into David's death. Carl Lee was so focused on Marie Delacroix that he wouldn't even consider any other possibility. Lucas wasn't going to ignore his training, his mind or his gut on this one. He owed David that much—if not more.

Lucas and the young police officer reached the glass door with Heaven Scent painted on it in a pastel arch. They were greeted by the smell of vanilla and the most beautiful woman Lucas had ever seen. The vanilla reminded him of his childhood. The woman reminded him he was a man.

"May I help you?"

Lucas felt rather than heard her voice. The soft, sultry drawl was so seductive that his thinking instantly went south. The woman standing before him exuded a kind of sensuality that seemed to grab him like a tracking beam.

Peltier stepped forward and introduced himself. "Lieutenant Peltier—New Orleans Police Department."

Lucas stood staring as she smiled at the young officer. She was small—no, petite was a better description. The hand she offered Peltier was laden with rings, and the numerous bracelets she wore jingled as they shook hands. It wasn't until her eyes found Lucas's that her brilliant smile faltered. Masculine pride swelled in his chest at her reaction, even though she recovered quickly.

Her eyes were neither blue nor gray, but a beautiful blending of the two. Her thick, feathery lashes were the same pure black as the mass of curls that spilled well past her slender shoulders.

"I'm Dr. Henderson," he said as he took her hand. It was warm and soft, and he couldn't help but wonder what the rest of her might feel like. "I'm the deputy coroner assigned to the David Markum case."

"That explains your aura," she said simply.

She sure doesn't look like a killer, he thought as

he glanced around the shop. But then neither did Ted Bundy, he reminded himself. "Aura?"

The smile she offered as she tilted her face to his was nothing short of heart-stopping. "Your body is giving off signals."

Is it ever!

"I have some tea brewed," she suggested, moving back behind the counter. "Can I pour you some?"

"No, ma'am," Peltier answered quickly.

Lucas rammed his free hand into the pocket of his jeans. Silently, he cursed Carl Lee long and hard. "I'm afraid this isn't a social call, Miss Delacroix."

She went about pouring the tea as if he hadn't said a word. She was one cool lady. He didn't like that. It wasn't a good sign. Most people would have reacted with more emotion. Innocent people ranted and raved.

Steam rose from the china cup she held with both hands. After taking a sip, she met his gaze. "I didn't kill David. Is this how Carl Lee plans to get to the governor's mansion?"

Lucas was taken aback by her frankness.

"We're only here to look around," Peltier said.

Lucas didn't need to read minds to know that Peltier had already found this woman innocent. That much was evident from the way he was adjusting his uniform and puffing out his chest. He was looking at Marie Delacroix as if she were some sort of door prize instead of a murder suspect. Even if those suspicions were pretty unlikely from the evidence so far.

"Carl Lee feels differently," she said, looking directly into Lucas's eyes. "Isn't that right?"

"The autopsy revealed that Mr. Markum did not die of natural causes."

"I see," she murmured softly. "The paramedics said it looked like a heart attack."

"It did," Lucas responded. It was his turn to do the staring. "But the toxicology screen turned up some inconsistencies. The coroner wants to be thorough."

She smiled again, and the gesture trapped his breath once more. "The coroner wants to be governor. What does he think killed David?" she asked.

Lucas shrugged and tried not to notice the way she looked when she spoke of David. There was an underlying familiarity that hadn't missed his notice. Then again, there was very little about this woman that had escaped his keen eye. Turning his attention to the rack of oils displayed on the counter, he asked, "Why don't you tell me what you did for Mr. Markum while the officer looks through your store? You don't object to the lieutenant having a look around, do you?"

"I have nothing to hide, Doctor," she answered easily, though he thought he saw a flash of annoyance mar her otherwise perfect features. "The treatment room is in the back."

Lucas handed his test kit to Peltier before he turned back to focus on the woman. Actually, he focused on the university diploma framed on the wall directly behind her, where she stood sipping her tea.

"Tulane?"

She nodded.

"I thought about going to Tulane, but I'm sure that was long before you were a student there."

Leveling her eyes on him, she said, "Really?"

He was pretty sure she was trying hard to convey disinterest. Too hard. Lucas had to admit that he wasn't used to that reaction. He wasn't conceited; the knowledge came from experience. Experience told him that mothers were still counseling their daughters to marry doctors.

He frowned. "I take it David never mentioned me?"

"Not a word." Marie took another sip of tea, then placed the cup on the counter. "Is there some reason he should have?"

Yes! "No," he answered. "Were the two of you friends?" He really wanted to ask if they had been lovers.

Her smile faltered, revealing just a hint of vulnerability. The hint was enough to make Lucas even sorrier that he hadn't told Carl Lee to do his own dirty work.

"You didn't come here to make small talk with me, Dr. Henderson."

He flashed a grin, hoping to get rid of the tiny worry lines that had appeared at the corners of her full, pouty lips. This wasn't going well. Nope, not at all. Once Peltier had the results of the field test, he would approach Miss Delacroix his way. "I'm sorry that I have to put you through this."

"Are you? You don't impress me as the kind of man who would do something that violated his conscience."

He hated the heat he felt on his face. "It wasn't my idea, believe me."

She lowered her gaze. "Perhaps."

"You don't have anything to worry about." Lucas forced himself to stop staring at her, opting instead to take a quick inventory of the various bottles at his fingertips. "So, what is a summa cum laude graduate of Tulane doing running a massage parlor?"

"This is an aromatherapy shop," she said with a definite chill in her tone. "I do therapeutic massage, give instruction in *feng shui* and try to educate people on alternative methods of healing and enhancing general well-being." Her expression became playfully defiant. "I also practice a little voodoo and some Wicca on the side."

He couldn't help but chuckle at the statement. "You didn't learn any of this crazy stuff at Tulane."

"You're right." She sighed. "But I did learn that traditional medicine wasn't for me. I discovered that when it comes to healing, instinct—intuition—can be a more powerful tool."

"No offense, but it doesn't take a whole lot of intellect to sell overpriced almond extract to tourists, claiming it will calm their dog or help them win at bingo."

"Right again, Doctor," she said. "Almond promotes intelligence and eloquence. Shall I wrap some up for you?"

Cocking his head to one side, he regarded her for a long minute. "You're quick, Miss Delacroix."

"Marie."

Just then, Peltier emerged from the back, holding a strip of litmus paper between his gloved thumb and forefinger. "Is this it?" he asked excitedly.

The paper had a greenish tinge where it was moistened. For some reason, Lucas didn't feel the elation he should have. The positive field test proved Carl Lee's theory. "Where did it come from?"

"Follow me," Peltier said. "You'd better come too, ma'am."

Pushing past the beads, Lucas found himself in a small room lined with shelves on two walls and heavy draperies on the others. The room was illuminated by at least two dozen white candles. The scent of cinnamon, sandalwood and cloves was almost overpowering.

"I'm burning incense to purify the room before my next client arrives," she explained with a nervous catch in her voice.

Something about her made him want to reach out and hold her, reassure her that there had to be some reasonable explanation for the results. But that wasn't an option.

Peltier pointed to an opaque glass jar on one of the shelves. After putting on gloves, Lucas retrieved the jar and pulled out the stopper.

"It doesn't smell like anything," Peltier told him.

"It isn't supposed to," she said as she came up beside Lucas. "There's nothing in there except jojoba oil. I use it as a—"

"Do they all contain the same thing?" he asked as he counted fifteen more jars.

"Yes. I mix in additional ingredients depending on the client's needs or complaints of pain." She got up on tiptoe and took a better look at the bottle he held. "Before you bother to ask, yes, that was David's base oil. See? Those are David's initials."

Carefully, he replaced the stopper and instructed

the officer to place the bottle and the field test strip into an evidence bag.

"Evidence of what?" she asked.

"Murder."

"Jojoba oil *cannot* kill," she informed him.

"It can when it is tainted with mercury salts."

She made a small disgusted sound. "That isn't possible. I get all my oils from a reliable source. I'm the only one in the shop who even touches the oils. There is no way any of these bottles could be tampered with."

Lucas looked at Peltier, then down at her. Either she was innocent or she was the best liar on the face of the earth. It didn't matter, really. It couldn't. It was no longer his problem.

"Arrest her."

"What!" she fairly screamed.

"Dr. Henderson," Peltier began in a low voice. "Do you know who she is? The Delacroix family owns most of Bayou Beltane. Her uncle is a state senator, her father is a federal judge...."

"And she killed David Markum."

CHAPTER TWO

"YOU'RE *WHERE?*" Shelby's astonishment carried over the telephone line.

Marie cradled the receiver with both hands, a necessity since her wrists were shackled with shiny chrome handcuffs. "I don't have much time," she told her sister. "The clerk recognized me so she let me out of the holding cell. Apparently she knows Daddy. You have to get here in the next hour. The judge has agreed to do the arraignment then."

"Let me call around," Shelby said. "I'll find a lawyer with experience in criminal cases."

"I don't want *someone*," Marie insisted. "I want you. It isn't as if I'm guilty. Just get over here before I end up spending the night in jail."

"I can't believe this," Shelby breathed. "How can this have happened?"

"Shelby," Marie said, sighing, "you're wasting time. But for the record, none of this would be happening if it weren't for Dr. Lucas Henderson. Please hurry."

Marie said goodbye, then handed the receiver back to the female officer with a waning smile. "Thank you."

"No problem, Miss Delacroix," the officer responded. "You can stay here until they call for you."

Marie was grateful. The few minutes she had been forced to spend inside that holding cell had been sheer torture. "Thank you, again."

From her seat next to the scarred metal desk in this small outer office, Marie had a partial view of the corridor, marred by steel bars with chipped paint the color of overcooked gumbo. At the end of the hall, she could see Dr. Henderson, and he didn't appear to be any happier about all this than she was, not if his steely expression and raised voice were any indication.

The officer looked at her with kind, dark eyes that reminded Marie of her friend and mentor, Desiree. "My aunt Suzanne comes into your shop all the time."

"Suzanne Ravenel?" Marie asked.

She nodded. "Aunt Suzanne says you have the best selection of aromatics in all of New Orleans. I know she'll be real upset when I tell her about your troubles."

"I didn't kill him," Marie said, struggling to keep her composure. The realization that she had been arrested, fingerprinted and photographed, and was about to be formally arraigned in district court on the charge of manslaughter, was slowly beginning to register. Her initial shock had evolved into fear, and now she was just plain mad. "It's all his doing," she added. She knew she wasn't being altogether fair, but on the other hand... Lucas Henderson might not be the driving force behind her arrest, but he was a handy target for her fury.

"Who?" the officer asked, placing her hands on her ample hips. "Dr. Henderson?"

"You know him?"

"He works down to Lakeview Community. My sister has a cousin from her first marriage who works as a lab technician there. When he came to the hospital about three months ago, it was all she talked about. We could be sitting in our Monday-night prayer meeting and she would tell us how he isn't married." A sparkle came to the woman's brown eyes. "Like she would have a shot at a man as handsome as him. And him being a doctor to boot."

"I thought I read that Dr. Carl Lee had ruled David Markum's death to be of natural causes," Marie said. "At least, that's what they printed in his obituary."

"Don't believe everything you read, sugar. Maybe it wasn't Dr. Carl Lee. You know he brought Dr. Henderson here 'cause he's some sort of fancy pathologist like that Quincy fellow from TV. He's testified a couple of times already. The single women in this building flock into the courtroom whenever he's on the stand. He sure is fine-looking. And I'd better go talk to him if we're ever going to get you out of here."

"I fail to see his appeal," Marie muttered, but she couldn't help glancing down the hall at him.

His height was the first thing she found to criticize. The man had to be six two or three. She was leery of tall men. Her father was tall, as was her brother. And though she loved them both, she knew from experience that tall men tended to be forceful and unyielding. Short and pleasant men were far easier to deal with. Men like David Markum.

Marie closed her eyes briefly, saying a prayer for her lost friend. When she opened her eyes again, an image of Lucas Henderson filled her vision. His hair was dark blond with sun-lightened streaks that suggested he spent time outdoors. She noticed his habit of raking his fingers through his hair, a habit she guessed would not be necessary if he took the time to have it styled properly so that it didn't constantly fall into his eyes. She remembered his eyes. They were hazel, with flecks of gold near the pupil—cat's eyes. No, the eyes of a predator. Sensual eyes.

If I'm lusting after the man who is partially responsible for my arrest, I'm losing it! Still, there was something about Lucas Henderson that seemed to draw her eyes inexorably to him. She couldn't have looked away if she'd tried. And she didn't try. Lucas was without question the most masculine man she had ever seen. His movements were graceful in spite of a healthy bulk of muscle. There was a sort of lazy maleness about him, and his worn jeans, crisp white shirt and conservative striped tie seemed to announce that he wasn't one to conform to anyone's standards but his own.

Marie couldn't help but smile at that thought. She knew firsthand what it was like to be a nonconformist in a den of traditionalism. She was only thankful she hadn't given in to family pressure and gone all the way through medical school before discovering that medicine wasn't her true calling. At least not the kind of medicine Lucas Henderson practiced.

A bubble of feminine laughter wafted down the hall as the young officer spoke with the deputy coroner, and Marie added "charming" to her list of adjectives for Dr. Henderson. It was obvious the woman wanted to prolong the conversation, but the doctor wasn't interested in the least. He didn't brush her off, not directly. He simply clasped her hand and offered that dazzling smile, then vanished down the hallway. Marie added "smooth" to her list.

The officer was still grinning several minutes later when she ushered Marie up the stairs to the courtroom, where Shelby was waiting.

"Are you okay?"

Marie almost gave in to her tears as her younger sister enveloped her in a hug. "It's hard to be okay when you've been wearing handcuffs," she answered, rubbing her sore wrists.

"When I went into law, I hadn't really planned on having to get my big sister out of jail."

"You can do it," Marie said, "can't you?"

Shelby nodded. "I hope so."

Hope?

"Judge Franklin went to law school with Daddy," Shelby told her. "I can't see him denying bail to one of Justin's girls."

"I didn't do anything to David," Marie stated as Shelby placed her briefcase on the floor next to the long table.

"It really isn't about guilt or innocence at this stage," Shelby explained.

"It is to me."

Shelby placed a comforting arm around Marie's shoulder. "I know you didn't kill anyone. What I'm trying to tell you is that this proceeding is just to determine if you're eligible for bail."

"If?"

Shelby winced. "I'm not handling this very well, am I. Listen," she went on in a soft, calm voice, "this

is just a formality. Since Judge Franklin offered to
hold your bail hearing immediately, I'd bet Beau's
favorite Armani suit that he's going to either dismiss
the charges or grant you reasonable bail.''

There was a commotion at the back of the courtroom and the two women turned to see their father,
Justin Delacroix, enter as if he were royalty. In a way,
he was. He represented the third of four generations
of Delacroix to practice law. The Delacroix were to
the law in Louisiana what the Kennedys were to politics in Massachusetts. Justin had recently been con-
firmed for a federal judgeship following a prestigious
career, and Shelby was now a lawyer in the family
practice in Bayou Beltane, the first woman in their
immediate family to graduate from law school.

Marie met her father's blue eyes, and that was
enough to breach the dam holding back her emotions.
She hurried toward him, and warm tears welled up,
then spilled down her cheeks as the tall, gracious man
pulled her into his arms. She might be twenty-nine,
but Marie felt like a small girl the instant her father
offered his comfort and his unconditional support.

''What idiot is responsible for this?'' Justin demanded as he stepped back and brushed the tears
from her face. ''I'll make sure he walks a beat for the
rest of his career.''

''The police have been very nice to me, Daddy,''
Marie said. ''I don't think they wanted any of this to
happen.''

''Then, is it the work of some new district attorney?'' Justin asked Shelby. ''Your grandfather and I
have a few enemies, especially since we expanded the
corporate division of the firm.''

"Daddy," Shelby interrupted, "I doubt this has anything to do with you or Grandfather. Unless you had some dealings with the deceased."

"I met Dr. Markum once. Some fund-raiser for the hospital. Uncle Philip was there—"

"I know you and Uncle Philip have your differences," Shelby said, "but even he wouldn't stoop so low as to kill a man."

Marie sensed something. It was just a flash, nothing she could really define, yet she had the impression that her father wasn't as convinced as Shelby that her great-uncle Philip wasn't somehow involved.

Drawing in a calming breath, she dismissed whatever she had sensed as nothing more than an extension of the longstanding feud between her grandfather, Charles Delacroix, and his twin, Philip Delacroix. It had been going on for so long now that she doubted even the principals remembered what event had caused the rift. Her great-aunt Mary and great-uncle William were neutral. Joanna, Philip's daughter, had crossed the battle lines and left her father's law practice to work for Marie's grandfather in Bayou Beltane. And Shelby occasionally was permitted into the enemy camp. The rest of the clan seemed to stick to their respective sides. The negative energy present on those rare occasions when the entire Delacroix family gathered always left Marie emotionally drained.

She watched now as her brother, Beau, entered the courtroom, followed by a stunning, auburn-haired woman. At first Marie thought they were together. A reasonable assumption, since Beau the Beautiful, a nickname coined by their sister Charly, was rarely—if ever—without the benefit of female companionship. But the woman slid into one of the long pewlike benches at the rear of the room. She was probably a reporter. The thought made Marie cringe. Her father didn't need this kind of negative publicity.

"Maybe you shouldn't be here," she suggested gently to him.

"Do you really think I could stay away when one of my own is in trouble?" Justin asked.

"You have to think of your career," Marie said. "I know your work is your life." *That's why Mother left you. She couldn't compete,* she added silently.

"My career isn't as important as my daughter," Justin assured her. "And you can bet that whoever is responsible for this abuse of the legal system won't have a career when I get finished with him."

"You'd be speaking of *that* person," Marie said, and pointed a steady finger at Lucas, who was standing on the far side of the courtroom, whispering rather vehemently to the newly arrived district attorney.

As if on cue, Lucas turned his head and looked at her with such compassion that Marie almost ran over and asked him why he was doing this if he had doubts. He had appeared much less sympathetic at her arrest earlier.

Shelby actually had to restrain Justin until Beau stepped up and led him to a seat behind the table where she and Marie would sit.

Shelby went to speak to the prosecutor while Marie told her father and brother what little she knew. "I'm not sure if this is Carl Lee's doing, or if Deputy Coroner Henderson is just trying to launch his own career."

"Did you sell him some potion that gave him hives?" Justin asked. "He looks as if he'd enjoy punching something."

"I never saw him before today, when he showed up at Heaven Scent."

"There's something going on here," Justin said after observing the man for a few minutes. "I'm a pretty good judge of people, and that man has an agenda."

"Are you sure you don't know him?" Shelby asked.

"I think I'd remember a man like him," Marie answered. "He doesn't exactly blend into the crowd. When he told the officer to arrest me, he also had them seal off my shop as a crime scene. He wouldn't even let me call my clients. I'll probably lose my business."

Shelby's face was tense with concern and her eyes deeply troubled. She handed Marie the crisp documents she held in her hand.

"You'd better have a look at these," Shelby suggested grimly.

"You don't believe any of this, do you?" Marie demanded once she had read the pages.

Shelby let out a wary breath. "It doesn't matter what I believe. What matters is what they can prove. Jeez, Marie," she groaned. "In a few short hours, the D.A.'s piled up some pretty damning evidence." She handed the documents to her father. "How are we going to get around the poison and Marie's fingerprints?" she asked him.

"Worry about that when the time comes," he answered. At that moment, the bailiff came out of a door to the right of the judge's bench. "Bail isn't about the evidence...thank God."

"All rise," the clerk called as Judge Franklin entered from a side door and climbed to his perch at the front of the room. "Case number 97-1119KMP. State of Louisiana versus Marie Justine Delacroix. Charges are violation of R.S. 14:31. Specifically, the defendant is charged with manslaughter in the death of David Markum, a human being, on or about December 5 of this year. The Honorable Gary Franklin presiding. Be seated."

Judge Franklin placed half glasses on the bridge of his slightly crooked nose before he skimmed the papers before him. Marie was shaking so much that her bracelets were jingling. She focused on the state seal above the judge's bald head, but she could feel a pair of eyes boring into her. She didn't need any psychic powers like Desiree's to know whose they were.

Justin and Beau took their seats directly behind the table where she stood with Shelby. Marie remained standing only because it seemed to be expected of her.

"Miss Delacroix," the judge began, "are you represented by counsel?"

"Shelby Delacroix for the defendant," Shelby said.

The judge offered a sad expression. "I'm quite pleased to have you in my courtroom, Shelby." His voice was soft, almost apologetic. "Congratulations on passing the bar. I knew you'd do your family proud, and I am sorry about the circumstances of your first appearance here."

"Your Honor," the prosecutor called, clearly annoyed. "Perhaps, given your obvious...familiarity…with the defendant and her family, it would be best if you recused yourself.''

That seemed to make the judge angry. ''You won't find a jurist in any parish in Louisiana who isn't acquainted with the Delacroix family. I know you are new to Orleans Parish, Mr. Griffin, so I'll ignore your inference regarding my partiality. Proceed.''

Marie sat down when Shelby gave a gentle tug on her arm. Her heart was pounding, and she would have given anything for a whiff of tangerine to give her the strength to deal with the inner turmoil she was experiencing.

Shelby remained standing and said, ''The defendant waives the reading of the charges and wishes to enter a plea.''

Judge Franklin nodded. ''The charge is manslaughter. How does your client plea?''

''Not guilty,'' Shelby said on her behalf.

District Attorney Griffin jumped to his feet. ''Your Honor, due to the heinous nature of the crime, we would ask that this defendant be remanded without bail.''

Realizing what it would mean if the judge granted the prosecutor's request, Marie started to turn to look at her father. Instead, she found Lucas watching her. His hazel eyes shimmered with some emotion she couldn't quite place. Pity, maybe? Great. That was just what she needed from the man who had almost single-handedly given Carl Lee the fuel for his little power play.

Marie glanced away quickly. Her father and brother offered her unspoken compassion, which seemed to fortify her with much-needed strength. Just before she turned back around, Marie again noticed the auburn-haired woman gazing at her from the rear of the courtroom. The intensity with which the woman stared made Marie wonder if she had been David's girlfriend. She vaguely recalled David mentioning something about a woman a few months back.

"As you know," Shelby began, "Miss Delacroix has strong ties to the community. She owns a business in New Orleans and presents no risk for flight. Miss Delacroix has no prior criminal record, and we would respectfully request that she be released on her own recognizance."

Griffin cleared his throat. "With all due respect to Miss Delacroix, er, the lawyer, not the defendant, the nature of this crime and the irrefutable evidence against this defendant—"

"Has the D.A. already won a conviction?" Shelby snapped sarcastically.

"She has a point, Mr. Griffin," the judge said. "I've never known a Delacroix to run from a fight. Bail is set in the amount of five thousand dollars. I'll set this matter in for the second week in January unless I hear differently from counsel. Have a nice holiday." The judge's gavel pounded once.

Marie had exactly three weeks of freedom.

CHAPTER THREE

DUSK WAS THREATENING as Lucas walked along the manicured pathway to the staff parking lot adjacent to Lakeview Community hospital. His anger over the mishandling of the Markum case was still fresh nearly twenty-four hours after the bail hearing. He'd given the D.A. more than enough scientific evidence to warrant the woman's incarceration, but it didn't *feel* right, and he couldn't get anyone to even hear his concerns. His attention was drawn to the sound of a car screeching to a halt just ahead of him, blocking the crosswalk.

It was a sleek, shiny green Porsche. A man emerged, his face shadowed by the light from the car's interior.

"May I have a minute of your time, Dr. Henderson?"

There was something familiar about the tall, brown-haired man, but Lucas couldn't place him. He'd met a lot of people in the three short months he had worked at Lakeview. Most were the political cronies of Carl Lee. He was exhausted, but knew it wasn't a good idea to blow off one of his boss's buddies.

Carl Lee had already basked in the spotlight of a press conference. His announcement that he had found strong proof of a murder *and* found the suspected killer was interesting, but apparently not as interesting as his second proclamation from the steps of the hospital. Announcing that Marie Delacroix was the suspected murderer had sent a ripple of shock and excitement through the small press corps. David Markum had suddenly become irrelevant.

"If it won't take too long," Lucas answered as he walked around to the driver's side of the car. "What can I do for you?"

"Can we go somewhere and talk—maybe I can buy you a drink?"

"I don't mean to be rude, but I've been here since four this morning. One drink and I'd probably fall asleep on the bar."

The man smiled at his remark. "Then, how about if we just grab one of those benches?" he suggested, pointing to a wooden bench along the landscaped pathway.

Lucas thought it was a little strange that the guy just left his car parked at that odd angle. Of course, there were a lot of things about his new community that he found unusual. A vision of Marie Delacroix's face flashed through his mind. Her image brought back a reminder of his lust, but there was something else, too. Nagging doubts that came from his gut. But that was crazy, and he chalked them up to lack of sleep.

"I need your help," the man said as soon as they were seated on the bench.

The scent of recently mowed grass hung in the humid evening air. It sure didn't feel as if Christmas was just around the corner. "What kind of help?"

"I need a good forensic pathologist," he answered. "I've been told that you're better than any in the city. You studied at Johns Hopkins, right?"

Lucas nodded, his interest mildly piqued. "I do mostly lab work here," he explained. "I'm a pathologist, but I did do some extra course work in forensics in Baltimore."

"Did you ever come across a case where a person was being framed for a crime?"

"Not personally, but I have read of several cases." Lucas rested his arm on the back of the bench and twisted so that he was looking at the man's profile. "Are you interested in having me consult on a case?" He tried to keep the excitement out of his voice. He wanted to come across as professional. Still, he would love an opportunity to do something more than staining tissue samples and shaving biopsies. The idea of being a consultant was appealing. He could continue to work in the lab, which he loved, but he would also have the chance to do more fieldwork.

"Actually, I was hoping I could get you to reevaluate a case."

Lucas stroked his chin. "I would need copies of all the reports, tests and statements from the case."

"You have them already."

"What are you talking about?"

"I want you to take another look at one of your own cases. I'll even pay your fee, if that's what it takes."

"Who are you?"

"Beau Delacroix. Marie is my sister."

"I CAN'T BELIEVE you talked me into this," Lucas said less than an hour later as Beau parked his car in front of a tony bar east of New Orleans.

"You've restored my faith in doctors," Beau said as they headed for the entrance. "I respect a man who is at least willing to listen to reason."

"Then steer clear of Carl Lee," Lucas cautioned. "I'll listen to what you have to say, then you hear me out. And Carl Lee is never to know about this, that's the deal."

The interior was long and narrow, with booths on one side and a bar on the other. Judging from the friendly wave Beau received from the barmaid, he was a frequent visitor.

A Cajun waltz played softly in the background as Beau selected the last booth. "They have the best gumbo in the parish here."

"I haven't yet developed a taste for gumbo," Lucas admitted as he scanned his place mat, which also served as a menu. He decided on a sandwich, then studied the man seated across from him. He was definitely Marie's brother. They had the same gray-blue eyes. In spite of the circumstances, Lucas had to admit that he found Beau a pretty likable guy. His easygoing demeanor and relaxed confidence were traits Lucas admired. He also related to the way Beau sweet-talked the waitress, who looked about fifty and flirted with the confidence of a happily married woman. *A man after my own heart.*

After they had ordered their food, Lucas took a swallow of his beer. "What do you do, Beau?"

"I manage the financial part of the family's holdings. I think that was one of the reasons my sister

Shelby became a lawyer. Jax, Marie, Charly and I sorta dropped the ball.''

"Jax?''

"Jacqueline. She's my twin. One hell of an equestrian,'' he added, pride evident in his tone. "She won a couple of bronze medals in Atlanta a year ago last summer. All of us but Shelby were a real disappointment to our father, who would have liked nothing more than to have all of his children study law.''

"Marie's career path must really have pulled his chain,'' Lucas said.

Beau shrugged. "Marie has always marched to a different beat. She really *tried* to do right by the family. She was premed at Tulane.''

Lucas's surprise must have been evident. Beau's smile grew wider, then he laughed as the waitress brought their food. "I see you made the mistake of thinking her diploma was just window dressing?''

"Guilty. I figured her for one of those liberal arts types. Maybe even women's studies,'' he admitted softly. "What happened?''

Beau's affable expression sobered slightly. "Most people who don't know her get the wrong impression of Marie. She's probably the smartest one in the family. Too smart to kill anyone.''

"The evidence doesn't say that,'' Lucas said as gently as possible. "I respect the fact that you want to help your sister, but I have to tell you, the tests I ran on the oils from her shop were an *exact* chemical match to the poison in David's tissue samples.''

"David?''

"We were roommates in college,'' Lucas explained.

"Now I understand why you went after her with such a vengeance," Beau said. "But you're way off base. There has to be some other explanation, because there is no way Marie could kill anything or anyone. Speaking of which, have you got a theory on motive?"

"First off, it wasn't my idea to go after her." Lucas took a breath and let it out slowly. "I don't think the D.A. has to provide a motive in order to get a conviction."

"That might be true, but the man's death would make a little more sense if we knew why he was killed."

"Maybe Marie and David were...involved."

Beau's smile returned. "I didn't know your friend was a loser."

"He was a psychiatrist," Lucas answered. "David was a great guy. Definitely not a loser. What do you mean by that?"

Beau laughed. "Marie only attracts losers. It's as if she has some sort of magnet attached to her back or something. Forget I mentioned it."

"But she's so beautiful."

Beau's affable disposition vanished. Immediately their eyes locked, and Lucas knew he was getting a warning even before the other man spoke.

"Careful, Dr. Henderson. We are talking about my little sister here."

"I just find it hard to believe that a woman who looks the way she does would attract losers."

"You don't know Marie. She spends most of her time trying to solve other people's problems. You might not believe in her kind of therapy, but I've seen it work. I know as surely as I'm sitting here that she is incapable of taking a life. Marie isn't like the rest of us, unless you count her temper.''

"Temper?"

"Vicious,'' Beau swore.

"What do you mean about the rest of you?"

Beau ordered them another round. "Marie always tries to do what's right.''

"And you don't?"

Beau's eyes twinkled as if he were a mischievous boy. "I'm at my best when I'm doing my worst. Jax is cool and elegant. She always knew what she wanted. She first sat a horse when she was four years old. Nothing could have deterred her from a career that had to do with horses.''

"Is she pretty?"

Beau grinned. "Stunning, but she's my sister, too, so you can look but don't touch.''

"Jax may have a different idea.''

Beau laughed. "Jax would chew a city boy like you into tiny pieces. The man who gets Jax will have to share her with horses, and you don't impress me as the type to share.''

"You've got a point there.''

"As for Shelby, family's all-important with her.''

"She's also a lawyer,'' Lucas grumbled. "I would never get messed up with a lawyer. Even an attractive one.''

"Good thing, because Travis—the love of her life—would rearrange your face if you even breathed in Shelby's direction. Charly would back him up, and I should warn you, she carries a gun.''

"Charly?"

"Short for Charlotte," Beau supplied.

Lucas saw the way his face softened. "What special quality does this sister have? Besides beauty—I'll assume that's a given."

"Charly isn't really a beauty. Not yet, at least."

"Prepubescent?"

"Pre-first-love."

"I don't follow."

"Charly wanted to become a cop because her passion is justice. There will come a day when my baby sister discovers other passions, as well."

"Want me to help her out there?"

"Want to die?"

Lucas laughed and raised his hands in mock surrender. "I've made a career out of staying away from ladies with protective big brothers." Lucas lifted his beer to his lips, keeping his glance trained on his companion. "Are you going to tell me about Marie?"

"Depends."

"On?"

Beau got that protective look in his eyes again and regarded Lucas for a long moment. Lucas didn't back down from the little ritual. "It depends on what you're thinking."

"I'm thinking that she's in a lot of trouble," Lucas said. "Finding the poison in her shop was a pretty damning bit of evidence."

"Tell me about the way you were looking at her in court yesterday."

Lucas took a drink. "She is a beautiful woman."

"I know. But Marie is a lot more than a pretty face."

"Such as?"

Beau seemed to study him for a few minutes, then came to some unspoken decision. "Marie is an invitation to seduction."

Lucas almost choked. "She's your sister."

"Don't I know it," Beau explained. "And Marie doesn't even realize the effect she has on men. Believe me, I spent a great deal of my misspent youth punching guys out for thinking exactly what you were thinking when you saw her for the first time."

Lucas was saved by the bar's dim lighting. He was pretty sure he was blushing for the first time since his high school days. "That must have been a full-time job."

Beau sighed. "My only reward for looking out for my four sisters was their friends."

"Their friends?"

"Pool parties, slumber parties—heaven can't be as wonderful as a houseful of nubile young bodies and adolescent fantasies."

"Sounds rough."

"I muddled through it. But I meant what I said earlier. Marie believes in what she does, and she believes in the basic goodness of people. Her only fault is being too spontaneous. She usually acts first and thinks about it later."

"Has she thought of a way to explain the poison?"

"We can't," Beau admitted. "I was hoping you could."

"Marie said something about being the only person who ever touched the oils. If that was true, then I can't think of a logical explanation for how mercury salts ended up in the bottle."

"Did you find the poison in any of the other bottles?"

Lucas hesitated. The prosecution would have to turn the information over to Marie's lawyer, anyway, so he shrugged and said, "No. We're checking on other outlets, but mercury salts are used in jewelry production, so you can imagine the amount pouring in and out of the Quarter."

"Have you considered that whoever did this wanted to kill your friend *and* frame Marie for the crime?"

"No."

Beau pushed his plate aside and folded his arms on the table. "If someone was after Marie only, that person would have tampered with all the oils. Since only your friend's oil was poisoned, it would seem to me that the killer's goal was to hurt David Markum and only David Markum—and implicate Marie."

Lucas suddenly wasn't hungry, and he definitely wasn't tired anymore. In fact, his brain was whirling as possibilities raced through his mind. Unfortunately, he couldn't come up with a plausible explanation for what had happened. At least not one that cleared Marie.

Beau reached into his pocket and peeled off some bills, tossing them on the table. "Are you up for a quick field trip?"

"Where?"

"I think I should tell you a little bit about Marie's aromatherapy."

"That probably isn't a good idea."

"Funny," Beau said, "Marie feels the same way."

CHAPTER FOUR

"Now isn't the best time, Nikki," Marie said gently as she leaned against the doorjamb.

Nikki Gideon simply shrugged her shoulders beneath the weight of the backpack that was as much a part of the sixteen-year-old as her baggy jeans and her cropped T-shirt. "This is the *perfect* time, Marie. I've decided to stay with you until this mess is fixed."

Marie took a deep breath, then followed the willowy young woman into her apartment. Nikki deposited herself and her backpack on the sofa. Marie searched the girl's face, then asked, "What is this *really* about?"

Nikki was transformed from poised young woman to pouting child in a matter of seconds. "Can't you believe that I came here to cheer you up?"

Marie smiled patiently. "Nice try. Does your mother know where you are?"

"My mother doesn't know anything," Nikki huffed. "She treats me like I'm three. She's so busy with her work that she doesn't care about me."

Marie sat next to the girl, not sure of the best approach. "That isn't true and you know it."

"But it is! That's why I've decided to move in with you."

Marie felt her eyes grow wide and it was only with

a great deal of effort that she was able to keep her jaw from dropping. "Move in? Here?"

Nikki looked at her with eyes full of hope. "Of course. You're in trouble, and I heard my mother tell Shelby that it wasn't a good idea for you to be alone right now."

Marie twisted a lock of hair around her finger. "It also isn't a good time for me to be responsible for a teenager."

Nikki looked scared. "You can't toss me out!" she wailed. "I don't have anywhere else to go!"

Rubbing her hands over her face, Marie tried to think. "I've got a lot on my mind," Marie began. "It wouldn't be fair to you if I—"

"Please," Nikki whined. "I just can't go home. I told my mother I wasn't coming back until…"

Marie looked at the girl. "Until what?"

Nikki's gaze dropped to the floor. "Until she stops trying to come between Etienne and me."

"All this is over a boy?"

"Not just any boy," Nikki answered. The girl's face positively glowed as she spoke. "Etienne and I are soul mates. We really understand each other."

Soul mates? Marie thought. "Are you sure you want to let a boy come between you and your mother?"

Nikki went back to pouting. Tracking her mercurial emotions was giving Marie a headache.

"I won't be any trouble," Nikki insisted. "I can help you in the shop and—"

"The shop is still closed," Marie said with a heavy sigh. "What about school?"

"I can miss the next couple of days. We don't do much before Christmas break."

"I only have one bed," Marie argued. "I've got—"

Marie's voice was silenced by a series of loud raps on her door. Glancing at the clock above the old fireplace, she wondered who would come calling so late.

"If that's my mother, I don't want to speak to her!" Nikki called.

Marie swallowed her groan and opened the door. She smiled at Beau's face, but the smile faded when she caught sight of the tall man behind him. "Why on earth would you bring *him* here?"

"Lighten up," Beau warned as he bullied his way into the apartment. "Hey Nik, what are you doing here?"

Marie only half heard the conversation behind her. She was having trouble taking her eyes off Lucas Henderson. The fact that her life was in total shambles was partly his fault. So it made absolutely no logical sense that she found him so intriguing. Morbid curiosity, she decided. The same curiosity that made people slow down to stare at the carnage of a traffic accident.

Only traffic accidents didn't have broad shoulders, a tapered torso and glittering hazel eyes.

"Miss Delacroix," he said with the slightest inclination of his head.

Even that small act caused his dark blond hair to fall forward into his eyes. Marie ignored the urge to reach up and brush it back into place. She had more pressing things to do—like swallowing the lump that had formed in her throat.

"Why are you here?" she asked, each syllable dripping with her contempt.

"Marie…" Beau warned. "Don't undo what has taken me hours to accomplish."

"What are you talking about?" she asked as she turned to face her brother. "Stop unpacking, Nikki. We need to finish discussing your options."

The teenager shrugged and stopped pulling hastily folded items from her backpack. "I'm not going back."

Marie's apartment seemed small with Nikki, Beau and Lucas crammed into it. "Beau?"

Nodding, Beau reached into his pocket and pulled out some money. Handing it to Nikki, he said, "How about running across the street and getting us some café au lait and beignets?"

"It's too late for her to be running around town," Marie said.

Nikki got a defiant look in her eyes before she snatched the money from Beau and stormed from the room. "I'll go with you!" Marie called.

"We need to talk," Beau insisted, grasping her arm. "There's a few thousand tourists in the Quarter and half that many cops. Nikki will be fine."

"What if Joanna calls?"

"I'm more concerned with getting the charges against you dropped."

Marie shrugged. "Unless you've found the real killer, I doubt your *friend* will listen to reason."

Lucas stared at her with amused eyes. "You did mention that your sister had a volatile temper."

Marie tilted her head back to meet his gaze. "I'm having a bad night. My teenage cousin thinks she can move in here, and thanks to you, my shop is still cordoned off as a crime scene—not to mention the reporters prowling around. Do you have any idea what the rents are like here in the French Quarter? I'll be lucky if I only lose my shop and my inventory.''

''I'll take Nikki home with me,'' Beau said. ''Odelle and Dad will see that she stays out of trouble until she and her mother work out whatever this is about.''

''Thanks,'' Marie said, giving her brother's arm a gentle squeeze. ''Do you have an equally simple solution to the manslaughter charges hanging over my head?''

Beau smiled broadly. ''Yes.''

''I'm all ears.''

''I've hired Lucas to find the killer.''

''He thinks he already has,'' Marie reminded Beau. ''He proved that when he had me arrested. Why do you think he'll help me now?''

Beau put his arm across her shoulder. ''Because I'm paying him.''

Marie's eyes narrowed as she studied Lucas's bemused expression. ''Isn't that some sort of conflict of interest?''

He didn't answer immediately. At least not verbally. His eyes fell to her mouth, then boldly touched every inch of her body. ''*Conflict* might be the right word.''

Testosterone levels soared as Beau stepped forward. Marie grabbed his shirtsleeve. ''Don't do it,'' she warned. Beau had this annoying habit of punching any man who looked at a Delacroix female with anything even close to impropriety. And impropriety was a tame description for the look in Lucas's devastating eyes.

"I'm not paying you to come on to her."

Lucas's smile was slow and meaningful. "No need to worry, Beau. Not yet, at least."

Beau took a menacing step forward.

"Stop it this instant," Marie snapped. "The two of you are acting like dogs fighting over a bone. I'll assume you were acting in my best interests," she told her brother. "But this is not a workable idea."

"I thought you were anxious to clear your name," Lucas commented. The challenge was there in his eyes.

Marie met his challenge and raised it a notch. "I thought you were anxious to make a name for yourself."

Beau became invisible.

"You thought wrong."

"So you're switching sides now?" she taunted. "Afraid you'll go down in flames when I'm found innocent?"

"I just want the truth."

"You might have considered that before you had me arrested."

"How do you know I didn't?"

Marie's spine stiffened. "Sorry, I just assumed that any person with so much as an ounce of character would not sit idly by while they ruined another person's life."

The muscles at his jaw tightened, and a look both dark and faintly dangerous came into his eyes as he headed for the door. "That one was free, Miss Delacroix. If you attack me again, expect consequences."

Lucas punctuated the remark by glancing over at her brother. It was as though he was almost daring Beau to comment. Amazingly, Beau didn't say a word. Not until after Lucas had left her apartment and his footsteps faded in the distance.

"What were you thinking?" Marie demanded. "That man was responsible for my arrest, you jerk." She balled her fist and punched his shoulder.

"Ouch," Beau cried with exaggeration.

"What!" Marie demanded when she saw that familiar humor sparkling in his eyes. "What is so funny, Beau?"

"You."

She fell onto the sofa and clutched a pillow to her breast. "Being accused of murder has made me a regular laugh riot."

Beau sat beside her, then gently tugged her closer so that her head rested against his shoulder. Marie felt some of the tension begin to recede.

"You need someone like Lucas, Marie."

She made a disgusted sound. "You need therapy."

He laughed. "You aren't getting any younger, kid. Thirty is looming on the horizon."

"Can you still see the horizon at your advanced age?" she asked after she had swatted him with the pillow.

"I'm a man."

"Aren't you supposed to pound your chest while swinging from a vine when you say that?"

"I'm serious, Marie. Lucas is a decent guy, and the two of you have a lot in common."

Marie felt her jaw drop. "My life is going to hell because of him. I guess that does give us something in common."

Beau squeezed her shoulder. "It wasn't his idea."

"Could have fooled me."

"You aren't the only one with a vested interest in this. Markum and Lucas were friends."

"Which means he'll work twice as hard to see me in jail."

"Something tells me Lucas would like to see you someplace other than jail."

Marie felt her face flame. "You're delusional, Beau." Her mind flashed an image of Lucas Henderson standing at the edge of her bed wearing nothing but that incredibly sexy smile. "Or maybe I am."

"I hadn't counted on him reacting to you like that."

"Reacting like what? The man barely said a dozen words."

"I saw his eyes. I know that look. Hell, I've used that look a few times myself."

"A *few* times?" Marie laughed. "Is there a woman in Bayou Beltane that hasn't had the pleasure of your company?"

"A gentleman never tells."

"And you're such a gentleman."

"So I'm not," Beau admitted. "Which is why I'm sure that Lucas Henderson is interested."

"I'm not interested in him."

"Liar. I saw your face, too, Marie. I know when a woman is interested."

"I don't want to hear this," Marie said as she tried to get up. Beau easily and gently trapped her.

"You don't want to admit that you find the guy attractive."

"I never said he wasn't attractive. But extremely attractive men are pigs. Take you, for instance."

Beau tugged a strand of her hair. "I love women."

"That's the problem, Beau. You love all women. Any woman. Every woman. Which probably explains why you bonded with the good doctor."

"You wound me."

"Mention Lucas one more time and I will."

"I'll have to risk it because I need to tell you something."

Warning bells went off in her head. "What?"

"I told Lucas you'd meet him at the house in the morning. He wants to meet Desiree, and I said you'd be happy to escort him."

"Forget it."

"C'mon. You want to get this whole mess over with, don't you?"

"Of course, but that doesn't mean I want to do it in his company."

"Chicken."

"Am not."

"Are, too."

The two of them began to laugh as if they were still squabbling children.

Beau placed a kiss on the top of her head. "It's good to hear you laugh."

"It's good to laugh."

"So, are you going to let Lucas help you?"

"No."

"You need his expertise."

"That may well be, but I don't need his attitude."

"He probably doesn't need yours, either."

"I don't have an attitude, Beau."

"Prove it."

"Why are you ramming this guy down my throat? Where is your loyalty?"

"I am being loyal. I'm trying to get you to do what's best for you."

"Lucas is best for me?" she scoffed.

"You won't know unless you give him a shot."

"I'll shoot him, all right."

"I'm serious, Marie. Stop blaming him for Carl Lee's decision. The man has the skills and the knowledge to help figure out how and why you've been framed for murder. He might just be your only hope."

"Shelby would be touched by your overwhelming confidence."

"Shelby will do a great job with the legal stuff. You need Lucas to figure out the rest. Smooth your ruffled feathers and give the guy a break. Please?"

Marie drew her bottom lip between her teeth. *You need Lucas.* "I'll take him to see Desiree, but I won't promise anything beyond that."

"HE'S HERE!" Nikki called with adolescent enthusiasm. "He's really cute for an old guy."

Marie shook her head and refused to show any emotion. Especially when she was in the keen presence of Odelle, a woman who had worked in the Delacroix household since before Marie was born. Riverwood was home to Marie, or at least it had been until she'd declared her independence. Still, there was something comforting about the familiar sounds of the creaking wood floor and the welcoming scent of coffee drifting through the spacious rooms.

"I can't believe Mr. Beau talked you into this foolishness," Odelle muttered, glancing out the window. "'Sides, no good can come from a man who looks as fine as that one."

Marie felt her eyes being tugged in the direction of the window. After a few seconds of futile internal struggle, her curiosity got the better of her and she looked out at the driveway. Then she stopped breathing. Lucas stood next to a late-model convertible, legs crossed at the ankles, talking to Beau. He seemed completely relaxed.

"You going out with him?" Odelle asked.

"We're just going to talk to Desiree."

"You sure got mighty gussied-up for a trip into the swamp."

"I'm not dressed up," Marie insisted.

"Not much," Nikki teased. "You only tried on four outfits before you settled on that dress."

Marie offered the teenager a withering look before she swung her heavy purse over her shoulder. She took a brightly colored scarf, folded it into a triangle and wrapped it around her head with practiced precision. The scarf was more than a fashion statement. By twisting the ends of the scarf into a rope and wrapping it around her head, she had a decent chance of keeping her thick hair from becoming a tangled jumble of curls in the wind. Ready at last, she stiffened her spine and walked out to greet the enemy.

SHE MOVED WITH A KIND of grace that reminded him of royalty. The sheer floral print dress teased the curves of her body as it caught the morning breeze. The scarf should have looked silly, but somehow, on her, it looked exotic. Lucas tried not to think about the fact that Marie was a desirable, attractive woman who had a powerful effect on him. He needed to maintain his objectivity. He needed to approach the situation professionally. He needed to kiss her.

"Good morning, Miss Delacroix."

"Doctor."

"I feel a sudden chill," Beau said with a smile. "My sister must not have sniffed the right amount of vanilla for breakfast."

Lucas suppressed a grin when Marie's elbow delivered a well-aimed nudge directly into Beau's midsection. "Excuse my brother," she said tightly. "He was dropped on his head as an infant and never fully recovered."

"We should go," Lucas told her. "I have to be back at the hospital by one."

"I just remembered," Beau said. "I need the keys to your car, Marie. Shelby needs to use it because hers is in for service."

Lucas stood patiently, as Marie dug in her sizable purse to retrieve a hefty key ring. They stood mere inches apart, close enough for Lucas to detect the sweet fragrance that drifted up from her skin, close enough for him to study the gentle slope of her throat, the curve of her breasts. He nearly groaned as his fantasies kicked into overdrive. Why had he let himself be talked into this? There was no way in hell he could spend any amount of time with Marie and keep his hands to himself.

Beau took the car keys and headed back to the house. "Have fun," he called.

"Ready?" Marie asked.

More than ready, he thought, sure they weren't speaking of the same thing.

Lucas held the door as she slid into the passenger seat. In doing so, the skirt of her dress rode up, allowing him an unobstructed view of one shapely thigh. He took a deep breath. It was going to be a long morning.

Seating himself behind the wheel, Lucas turned to her. "I need directions," he said. "I haven't been out this way before."

Marie supplied the route, and they drove in an uncomfortable silence for a while. Finally she asked, "Why are you doing this, Lucas? If David was really your friend, isn't this like selling him out for a dollar?"

"David and I were good friends in college. I'm doing this because your brother can be very persuasive."

She seemed to stiffen in the seat. "Beau is a natural deal maker. How much is he paying you?"

Lucas shrugged. "Five hundred an hour."

She made a disgusted sound. "You're not worth that much."

"How would you know?"

"Because you had me arrested. As far as I can tell, you aren't the most competent person in the world."

"I'm not the one accused of murder."

"Manslaughter," she corrected him. "And as far as I'm concerned, this is a dumb idea."

"I gave Beau my word."

"And I'll tell him you were all set to keep it, but this just isn't a workable option."

"Why not?"

"Because."

"Because *why?*" he asked, bringing the car to a screeching halt in the middle of the flat dirt road.

She turned her gray-blue eyes on him. "Because we can't work together. I don't like feeling this tense."

Lucas studied her troubled expression. "If I'm willing to accept the possibility that you aren't responsible for David's death, why can't you accept my help?"

"Because it's your fault that I'm in this mess."

"Hardly. I tried to get Carl Lee to wait but he went to the D.A."

"Since you're not convinced I'm innocent, how can we possibly work together?"

"I have some doubts about your guilt."

"Some doubts? That's the best you can do?"

Lucas slammed his palms against the steering wheel, causing her to jump. "Beau was very persuasive, but there's still the matter of the physical evidence."

"That had to be planted," Marie insisted. "I didn't add poison to the oil."

"I need proof of that."

"*You* need?" she mocked. "I'm the one facing trial in less than three weeks."

"If we can prove that someone else tainted the oil, the charges will be dropped."

"Gee, and you went to medical school to figure that out?"

"Sarcasm doesn't become you."

"How would you know? You don't know anything about me."

"I know that you gave up a promising career in medicine to mix useless magic potions to sell to tourists."

Marie cursed him before her mouth snapped shut. Lucas was left with a racing heart and the rush of adrenaline that had been building during their argument. God, she was frustrating, infuriating...and desirable as hell.

The tires spewed gravel as he threw the car into gear and continued down the dirt road, an awkward silence stretching between them.

What is wrong with me? he wondered as they traveled deeper and deeper into the inhospitable swamp. He seemed to vacillate between thinking she could be a killer and just plain thinking about her. His hormones had never gotten in the way of his logic before, so what was it about Marie Delacroix that had him so screwed up?

Marie directed him to a small, weather-beaten pier where two boats were tethered by thick, water-stained ropes. "What are we doing?"

"You can only get to Desiree's by water." She smiled at him as her dainty fingers grasped the door handle. "You can row."

She stepped into the boat with practiced precision. Obviously she had no qualms about venturing into the hostile environment. As he reached the edge of the pier, he glanced down at the murky water. A snake skittered past, and some unknown insect or bird or something began to sing a rather ominous-sounding mantra.

The boat wasn't impressive, and he had to swallow the urge to ask her if it was seaworthy or swampworthy or whatever the term might be. A rusty motor had been pulled up out of the water. Marie stepped into the bow and sat down.

Lucas teetered slightly when the boat rocked from his weight. Genuine fear of whatever lived in the swamp kept him from pitching into the drink.

"Not used to this sort of travel?" Her back was to him.

"There is a lot of water in Maryland," he informed her as he took up the oars. He sat down and lowered them over the side. His first thrust sent the boat lurching forward, only to have it jerk backward.

"We'll get there faster if you untie the boat first." She didn't laugh out loud, but he saw her shoulders vibrate.

"Good tip." Lucas reached over and yanked the rope free from the mooring.

"Go that way," she instructed, pointing to the left.

After about five minutes, his shoulders and arms were screaming. He was using muscles he had never used before, and they were complaining en masse. The first beads of sweat trickled between his shoulder blades at about the same time that something big and ugly glided through the brown water a few yards from the boat. Ignoring his muscles, he rowed harder.

"Someone actually lives here?" he asked as he surveyed the ramshackle building perched on rickety pilings. A boat that looked just minutes from sinking bobbed on their wake at the pier. Lucas managed to coax their own boat behind it on the third try.

"Desiree and her family are almost a part of the swamp," Marie answered without emotion. "Not everyone needs a satellite dish and a microwave to feel fulfilled." She climbed out of the boat and pulled the rope taut so he could step up onto the pier.

Marie walked in front of him as they headed toward the house. Had she not told him someone lived there, Lucas knew he would have rowed by the building, thinking it abandoned. It appeared to be constructed from wood and vines, and only the glass in the windows and the door looked as if they'd come from a store.

The woman who emerged from the house wore a tattered dress and swamp boots. The shock of white hair contrasted with her café-au-lait skin. She was thin, but any notion of frailty didn't seem to fit. She turned her inquisitive brown eyes on him.

"Who have you brought with you?" she asked.

"Hi, Desiree," Marie said as she stepped up to give the older woman a hug. "This is Dr. Lucas Henderson. He needs to know a little bit about the base oils you supplied me with."

The woman kept eyeing him, her expression guarded.

"The same Dr. Henderson who had you arrested?" she asked, speaking in French. Lucas hid his amusement. There was no way the woman could know that he was fluent in the language.

"Beau thinks he can help," Marie answered in equally rapid-fire French.

"What do you think?" Desiree asked.

"I think he's easy on the eyes."

Ignoring the pungent scents coming from the shack, Lucas followed the two women inside. He looked around in awe, never having seen anything like Desiree's home before. There were jars, candles, feathers, furs and several types of plants, all interspersed with bones, beads and various talismans. There was also another woman seated in the four-room shack. Lucas took one look at her and knew that he was looking at Desiree's adult child. The resemblance was unmistakable, though the younger woman was lighter in complexion.

Desiree and her daughter began a rather heated and animated discussion in a dialect that he guessed was Cajun. Lucas took Marie's elbow and lowered his head to hers. "What is she saying?"

"Flora thinks you're here to accuse Desiree of the murder. She thinks her mother should put a curse on you and send you on your way."

"I've been cursed before," Lucas responded, slightly amused.

"I wouldn't make light of this," Marie cautioned. "I've seen Desiree's power at work."

"Are we talking voodoo here?" Lucas asked, chuckling softly.

The woman called Flora became more lively as she argued with her mother. Lucas watched the interchange, fascinated and a little confused. Whatever the cause of the disagreement, the end result was Flora shoving past him and stomping outside. He guessed she was furious. Anyone would have to be to go out into the swamp.

Desiree looked at him with searching brown eyes

that made the hair at the back of his neck stand on end. Lucas dismissed the reaction. He didn't put any stock in things like curses and chants. They had no basis in pure science.

Desiree said something to Marie in her native tongue, though she spoke more slowly.

"She wants us to sit down. She senses something."

"Impatience," Lucas muttered, but he followed Marie to a small, scarred round table flanked by rickety hand-caned chairs.

A thick, hand-fashioned candle burned in the center of the table, casting Marie in a soft light that made her dainty features appear exotic, almost otherworldly. Her eyes were wide, her cheekbones starkly defined, her full lips pressed together. Almost reluctantly, Lucas turned his attention back to the old woman. Desiree went to a cabinet and pulled a small velvet pouch from the cupboard. Carefully, she untied a tattered gold rope from the pouch and carried the open bag back to the table, where she took her seat.

For a long second, their eyes met. It was a bizarre experience, to say the least. Desiree made him feel as if she had the power to see into his very soul. He didn't like the sensation any more than he liked the swamp. "I'm a little pressed for time," he said.

"Hush," Marie whispered, reaching over and squeezing his thigh.

The feel of her small hand on his leg was enough to render him speechless, but his irritation at Desiree's ministrations overpowered the pleasant sensation of Marie's touch. He hadn't come all the way out into this godforsaken place to participate in some kind of backwoods séance. Enough was enough. "Look—" he began.

"Hush!" Marie admonished, only this time he wasn't treated to the feel of her hand. "Desiree needs to do a reading before she'll agree to talk to you."

"A reading?" Lucas repeated. "A reading of what? My palm? Tea leaves?"

"Bones," Desiree grunted as she spilled bleached and cracked bones onto a dented metal plate.

Lucas leaned over and whispered, "How will chicken bones help her answer my questions?"

"It isn't the bones. She just uses them to focus on while she gets in touch with her sight."

Lucas closed his eyes and stifled an impatient groan. "Then what do we move on to? Eye of newt?"

Marie glared at him, warning him to keep his sarcasm to himself. He was about to get up and leave, when Desiree began to speak.

"I sense bad things coming for both of you," she said as she stared into the flame of the candle before her. Her dark, gnarled fingers skated over the bones. "You don't have the faith yet," she continued in a soft tone, her eyes fixed on him. "But you will. It will come at a dear price, too."

"What price?" Marie asked.

Judging from her tone, Lucas was sure Marie was buying this carnival act hook, line and sinker. Beau wasn't paying him enough to sit through something as ludicrous as this. He scooted his chair back but stopped when Desiree's gaze caught and held him.

"The person who killed your friend has killed before. This person is close. Too close."

"Can you see the person?" Marie asked.

Desiree shook her head and her forehead wrinkled in deep concentration. "Too many shadows," she answered. "But trouble comes. So does..."

"So does what?" Marie asked urgently.

Desiree took her hands off the bones as if they had suddenly bitten her. All in all, Lucas thought it was a pretty good act. She'd probably make a decent living as a street performer in the Quarter.

"So does what?" Marie asked again.

"You must stay with him," Desiree instructed. "This man has your future. This man is your future."

"Tell me more about the killer," Marie pleaded. "Is it a man or a woman?"

Desiree shook her head sadly. "I have nothing more for you. I'm sorry. Maybe if you come again?"

"Please," Marie begged. "I don't even know where to start looking."

"How about the oils she supplied to you," Lucas suggested.

Desiree's entire demeanor changed. She closed her eyes and her head rolled back on her shoulders as she sucked in an audible breath. "Go!" she yelled. "The danger is close."

When Marie started to rise, Lucas grasped her arm. "We need the oils so I can run tests."

She looked frightened and exasperated, but she went to an area that might have been a kitchen and began searching through containers along the shelving. Lucas left the table where Desiree sat slumped over, and joined Marie.

"Do you know what you're looking for?"

"Base oil."

"I need Desiree to show me which of these she shared with you. I—"

"The blue jar," Desiree called weakly.

Glancing over his shoulder, Lucas was annoyed to see that the woman was still playing her part to the hilt. She looked exhausted and spent. If he had the time, he would have told the old woman what he really thought of all her smoke and mirrors.

"Go, Marie," she called out. "Watch out for the danger."

"What danger?" Lucas asked.

"The killer knows."

"Knows what?"

Desiree stared at him. "The killer knows Marie is searching, asking questions. She is getting close. You should get away for a while. Go someplace safe."

"I'll be careful," Marie promised, and walked over to give the old woman a hug.

"Stay with that man," she whispered, her piercing eyes focused on Lucas. "You're safe with him."

"Desiree is certifiable," Lucas grumbled several minutes later as they untied the boat and climbed in.

"You got what you wanted," Marie said.

Something in her distant tone made him glance at her. He was surprised to find her so pensive. Any rational person would dismiss the rantings of that old fool in an instant. Then he remembered that he was dealing with a woman who sold cinnamon for a living.

"You can't really believe all that junk."

"Desiree has a special gift."

"Yeah," Lucas agreed. "She's a hell of an actress."

"She isn't acting."

"You can't be serious."

"Just because you don't understand something, Doctor, doesn't make it any less valid."

"Reading chicken bones is valid?"

"I told you, she wasn't reading them to see. She focuses on them to clear her mind so that she can concentrate on her visions."

"I'm beginning to understand why your brother was so sure you couldn't plan a murder."

"What is that supposed to mean?"

"Exactly what it sounds like. David Markum was killed by someone who had enough intelligence to formulate a rather complicated scheme for murder."

"Are you implying that I'm stupid?" Marie asked.

"I can't give you too much credit if you're willing to buy into that old woman's dog-and-pony show."

"If I'm so dumb, how come you're rowing?"

"What?"

"Try dropping the engine, Doctor."

"If the engine works, why did you make me row this thing?"

Marie smiled at him with a devilish light in her storm-colored eyes. "Impulse. You made me mad so you had to be punished."

He gaped at her. "You were punishing me?"

She smiled. "Yep."

He leaned forward and grasped her shoulders, heedless of the rocking boat. "Careful, Marie, you might not like how I get even."

Feeling her shiver was enough—for now. He turned and lowered the engine into the water. Luck was with him and it started easily. He'd learned a lot during the little trip, he thought as they headed out of the swamp. But he also had a lot of new questions. First among them was why he wanted to take Marie Delacroix in his arms and see where it would lead them. He mulled over that thought during the boat ride back to the pier.

He and Marie barely spoke on the drive back to Riverwood. But as the car turned into the horse-shoe-shaped driveway in front of the Delacroix family home, Marie gave a cry of alarm. A police cruiser with flashing lights was parked in front of the house.

"Oh, my Lord!" she gasped.

"I'm sure it's nothing," Lucas said, trying to reassure her.

"See? Desiree was right to warn me," Marie cried. "I hope it isn't Daddy."

Lucas brought the car to an abrupt halt behind the police cruiser. Illuminated by the flash of red-and-blue lights, Marie bounded from his car.

Lucas raced after her, catching up with her on the third step from the top. They were met by Beau, who immediately grabbed Marie and said, "It's Shelby and Joanna."

"What?"

"There was an accident," Beau began.

"An accident?"

Beau nodded. "They're both fine—"

"What happened?" Lucas demanded, placing his hand at the center of Marie's back.

"According to Shelby, some jerk in an old four-door ran them off the road."

CHAPTER FIVE

LUCAS HAD BEEN KIND enough to drive her to Lake-view Community Hospital as soon as they had heard the news. He had left her in the emergency room with instructions to a rather harried nurse that she should be taken to her sister as soon as possible.

"Are you sure you're okay?" Marie asked Shelby as she looked for any signs of injury.

"I'm fine," Shelby insisted. "I don't even have a bruise. I'm really sorry about the car."

"Forget the car," Marie said. "I'm just glad you and Joanna are okay."

Shelby squeezed her hand. "Wasn't that Lucas Henderson I saw with you when you came in?"

Marie felt her cheeks warm. "He...gave me...a lift."

"Have you lost your mind?" Shelby demanded. "He's the major witness against you."

Marie shrugged. "That was before Beau got ahold of him."

Shelby's expression grew alarmed. "What did he do? Please tell me it was legal."

"It was. Lucas agreed to review the case...for a fee."

"You're *paying* him?"

"Beau is," Marie answered. "They have some sort

of agreement where Lucas only gets paid if he un- covers evidence of the real killer.''

"At least I can use this to discredit him when he takes the stand.''

"I think he really believes that I'm innocent," Ma- rie argued. "He might even be able to prove that my therapy didn't kill David. At the very least he might be able to give me a clue as to who is doing this to me.''

"It's still my job to discredit him any way that I can,'' Shelby said. "If I can make him look like a fool in front of the jury, we might be able to get the charges dismissed.''

Marie's mind was in overdrive. "But what if he can help me?''

Shelby sighed. "If you wanted to bring in a foren- sic specialist, you should have called me for a referral, not hired the state's witness. Have you thought about what could happen if he uncovers evidence that is contrary to your interests?''

"He seems pretty sincere.''

"Did you make that decision with your brain or some other part of your anatomy?''

Marie let out a long breath. "Maybe I should have told Beau I would think about it, huh?''

"I can't believe you and Beau would do something so potentially detrimental to your case, Marie! I swear, when the two of you get together, nothing good happens. I'd hoped that owning your own busi- ness would have taught you to think before you acted.''

"I'm sorry, Shelby. Beau can be pretty convinc- ing.'' *And Lucas Henderson is a very intriguing man.*

"You stay away from Dr. Henderson and I'll take care of our dear brother," Shelby promised. "I think you should steer clear of the deputy coroner. You can help him pick up the pieces after I shred him and his reputation during the trial."

Marie felt the weight of her sister's convictions. Shelby never did things in half measures. If she believed a member of her family was being threatened, she would defend him or her with every cell in her body. "I just thought of something I need to do. Will you hate me if I leave you now?"

Shelby shrugged. "I'm just waiting for Joanna. Beau's going to give me a lift home—assuming the administration ever discharges me from this place. Just remember—stay away from Henderson."

"I hear you," Marie said. After hugging Shelby, she followed the signs that took her down into the bowels of the hospital, where she knew she would find Lucas.

She didn't want to be responsible for Shelby ruining the man's career.

The smell of chemicals was strong, and the tap of her heels echoed off the painted cinder-block walls. Something about the deserted basement gave Marie the creeps, and she quickened her pace. Her trepidation did not ease any when she reached a door marked Morgue and heard the muffled sound of voices.

She was about to knock when the voices became louder.

"*You* ran the tox screen and *you* found the poison in her shop."

"So now I've got a few doubts."

"Lucas, son, you're going to make me look like a

fool. We've made the case against Marie Delacroix, now leave it alone."

"I'm telling you, it just doesn't feel right. I don't think she did it. Marie has no motive."

"Motive isn't our province, son. That's the D.A.'s job. Griffin can figure out why she killed him."

Marie recognized the unmistakable voice of Carl Lee Shivley.

"She could be guilty," she heard Lucas admit. "But I read Peltier's report about the accident."

"Accident? What in hell are you talking about now?"

"Shelby and Joanna Delacroix were in an accident."

"What does that have to do with Markum's murder? He didn't die in an accident."

"You know the Delacroix," Lucas said. "Shelby was driving Marie's car."

"How does an accident play into the Markum matter?"

"Shelby and Marie look an awful lot alike."

"I know Shelby. She and Marie are as different as night and day."

"I'm not talking personalities. I'm just saying that it's a little too coincidental that Shelby was run off the road while driving Marie's car. What if the person responsible was trying to hurt Marie?"

"I think your little visit to Desiree Boudreaux bent your brain, son," Carl Lee snorted. "You had no business going out there. Most folks in the parish believe in her, but not me. And I'd venture a guess that you don't, either."

"I never said I believed her. I'm just saying we

should reexamine the evidence. Something about this whole case is wrong. I feel it.''

"Know what I think?'' Carl Lee asked.

"What?''

"I think you spent time with little Marie and what you're feeling doesn't have a damned thing to do with this case. Not that I can say I blame you.''

"Watch it,'' Lucas warned in a tone that gave Marie a chill.

"If you want to keep your job here, you'll stay away from the Delacroix. If I hear you've gotten within a hundred yards of that girl before the trial, consider yourself fired.''

Marie managed to slip into a nearby closet just as Carl Lee stormed from the morgue. She waited until the sound of his footsteps faded before she entered the morgue without knocking.

Lucas was seated in front of an expensive-looking piece of equipment. He didn't look up immediately, giving Marie an opportunity to study him. His hair was disheveled, as if he'd been raking his square-tipped fingers through it. A long white lab coat hung from his broad shoulders. Soft denim jeans hugged his powerful thighs. A radio was on somewhere, playing an aria that she could not have named if her life depended on it. With one foot, Lucas absently kept time to the complicated music.

Marie cleared her throat.

Nothing.

She cleared it again.

Still nothing.

"Did you mean what you said to Carl Lee?''

Lucas lifted his head with a start, turning his amber-flecked eyes on her. Rimmed with dark lashes, his hazel eyes still flickered with traces of residual anger.

"What?"

"I heard your argument."

"He thinks I might put his political butt in a sling."

Marie smiled. "Shelby just reamed me along the same lines."

"So she's all right?"

"Yep. Joanna, too."

"I'm glad to hear it."

A palpable tension filled the few feet that separated them. Marie was so confused at this point that she wasn't quite sure why she had come to see him.

"Is there something I can do for you?"

Marie looked down at the cracked tile floor. It seemed easier to talk to him when she wasn't gazing into those incredible eyes.

"I came down here to tell you that Shelby will tear you to shreds when you take the stand at my trial."

"Echoes of Carl Lee."

Marie smiled. "I haven't ever told you that I was sorry about David. I know he was your friend."

"He was indeed."

A strange lump came to her throat when she glanced up to see the pain in his eyes. "I know you were willing to help me and I appreciate the offer, but I can't be responsible for costing you your job. I'll work on Shelby so you won't be embarrassed when we go to court. I'm sorry you got into trouble with Carl Lee."

Lucas swung his large frame around in the chair and rose to his full height. Taking only two strides, he stopped just in front of her. He smelled faintly of cologne and coffee. It was a definitely masculine mixture that seemed to reach out and touch her.

"I'm not in trouble. As a staff pathologist, I have a contract here. Carl Lee probably won't do anything more than threaten me, Marie."

The sound of her name on his lips caressed her ears.

"Not yet, at least. I'll explain to Beau," she offered.

"Try explaining to me, first."

"What?" she said.

He ran his hands through his hair and took a long breath, letting it out slowly. "You raced down here to warn me about your sister. Why?"

"Because I don't like to be the cause of problems."

He smiled. "No other reason?"

"No." The word came out like a croak as his finger traced the line of her jaw.

"I don't believe you."

"I'm already accused of murder. Just tack on lying." *Stay cool*, she told herself. Only she didn't feel cool. In fact, the room was warm. No, not the room. The heat was coming from him.

"All the evidence points to you." His fingers slid along the side of her throat.

Marie was nearly lost in the hypnotic softness of his deep voice. "Someone would like for you to think that."

He nodded. "Do you have the kind of enemies that would go to such elaborate lengths to put you in jail?"

His fingertips grazed the flesh along her neck, setting little fires in their wake. "I don't have any enemies that I know of." *When you touch me, I don't think I know my name.*

"Why would a total stranger frame you?"

"If I knew that, I'd know who the killer was."

Lucas sighed and stepped away slowly, his hand slipping to his side. "Is there anything else?"

Without bothering to think through the ramifications, Marie said, "I still want your help."

"You heard Carl Lee."

Marie reached out and grabbed a handful of his coat. "I know this is asking a lot, but Desiree said that if I stayed with you, things would work out."

His expression hardened immediately. "You only want my help because of what Desiree said?"

"It isn't just Desiree," Marie amended quickly. "I need your scientific knowledge."

"Any chemist can test the base oil."

"But any chemist wouldn't have the same effect on the jury. If I can prove my innocence to you there's no way I'll be convicted."

"How do you plan to do that?"

"C'mon, Lucas. There's a part of you—deep down—that knows I didn't kill David. I've seen it in your eyes."

His smile was breathtaking. "What if I told you that what you see is good old-fashioned desire."

"Excuse me?" Marie asked in a helium-high voice even she didn't recognize.

Lucas shrugged. "I find I have a very strong attraction to you."

Blinking once, Marie felt panic swell in the pit of

her stomach. "Well...um...thank you, of course. I'm flattered and—"

He chuckled softly. "I'd say you were flustered."

Marie began backing toward the door. "I'm flattered, really. I should go and see if my sister's left. Bye."

Great going! she chided herself as she raced back up the stairs. *Since when do you run from a man because of a compliment? He must think I'm a complete bozo now.* She grimaced. *I know I do.*

"You're moping."

Lucas looked up as Beau took the stool next to him at the bar. He wasn't in the mood for company. He should have handled Marie differently. He'd pushed too hard, too fast, and scared her. "Go away," he grumbled, lifting the neat Scotch to his lips. The drink burned a path from his throat to his stomach.

"Delacroix never give up."

"I thought that was the Little Engine That Could."

"Cute," Beau said before ordering himself a beer. "I saw Marie."

"So did I."

"Want to tell me why she's blushing and stuttering?"

Lucas met the other man's eyes. "Not particularly."

Beau gave him a resigned nod. "She didn't have much to say, either. At least, not about you."

"Is that supposed to mean something to me?"

Beau took a sip of his beer, then hugged the long-neck bottle between his palms. "She's decided to investigate on her own."

"That isn't real smart."

"I agree," Beau said. "But once my little sister gets something in her head, she's like a dog with a bone."

"Why are you telling me this?"

Beau tipped the bottle to his mouth and drank a decent portion of the beer. "Just making conversation. I know you probably won't care to know that she's decided to go to Markum's apartment to look around."

"But the cops have already been there."

Beau stared long and hard at Lucas, his expression inscrutable. "Desiree told her to start there."

CHAPTER SIX

I'M FLOATING, she thought. *Floating away...*

"Lie still." She heard the command and struggled to open her eyes.

"My throat..." Marie began coughing, then sucked in great gulps of air while strong arms held her. "Why does my throat feel like it's on fire?"

"Gas."

She gasped a few more times before her heavy eyelids finally opened. "Lucas?"

"I'll go call an ambulance."

"No!" she insisted as she grabbed his arm. "I'll—I'll get into trouble for breaking into the apartment."

"It would serve you right," he said with a playful smile.

Sitting up, Marie realized that she was out on the balcony of David's apartment. Lucas helped her get to her feet, keeping an arm around her so that she had no choice but to lean against his powerful body. If a gas leak had caused her to lose consciousness, then being held against Lucas Henderson would probably kill her! "I'm okay, I just—"

"What?"

Marie tensed as the memories came flooding back. "I was in the bedroom."

"The kitchen," he corrected her. Turning her to face him, he began examining her pupils. "The cops must have accidentally turned on the burners of the stove when they were searching the place, and the pilot light was out. I can't believe you didn't smell the gas when you came in."

"The gas wasn't on when I got here," she assured him. "Whoever hit me must have turned it on."

"Someone hit you?"

In response, Marie took his hand and guided it to the tender lump on the back of her head. When she saw him wince, she knew she hadn't imagined any of it.

"We should call the police."

"No police," Marie insisted. "I don't need any more trouble than I already have. Besides, I'm fine now."

"You could have a concussion, and you should be on pure oxygen to get rid of the gas in your lungs."

"Can't you take care of that?"

"I don't usually carry a tank of O_2 in my car."

"I'll take deep breaths," she said. "I'll make some sandalwood incense when I get home. That will take care of my lungs."

"You want to tell me what happened here?" Lucas asked.

"I was in the bedroom," Marie began, moving away from him. "I had just found the notebook when I felt a sharp pain explode in my head. That's the last thing I remember."

"Any idea how long you were out?"

"What time is it now?"

"Almost half past eleven."

"No more than fifteen or twenty minutes."

"That's good," Lucas said. "You couldn't have inhaled much gas in that short amount of time."

"The notebook!" Marie cried, racing back into the apartment. Even though Lucas had opened all the windows, the smell of gas still hung in the air. She felt mildly queasy, but she remained focused as she reentered David's bedroom. "It's gone!" she exclaimed in dismay

"What is?" Lucas asked, coming up behind her.

"It was right here." She pointed to the now empty drawer in the nightstand. "David's appointment book. It covered the entire year."

She felt Lucas's hands on her shoulders, then he gently turned her. Catching her chin with his thumb and forefinger, he tilted her head back and met her gaze.

"What was in this notebook?"

"Names, dates, notations and some numbers that didn't make any sense. Now it's gone. I only had a chance to study a few pages before he hit me."

"You saw him?"

Marie shook her head. The action caused her to brush against his warm fingers, making her acutely aware of his touch. One hand held her chin while the fingers of the other were splayed at the small of her back. If she stepped forward just a fraction of an inch, she would be able to feel the entire length of his body.

Marie backed away from him, needing the distance to quell her fantasies. The temptation to touch him was great, but it was probably the result of the knock on her head. She had to stay focused where Lucas was concerned.

"Did you see anything?" he prompted.

"No."

"Then how do you know it was a man?"

"I don't," she said. "I guess I was just assuming it was a man since women don't usually rely on brute force to make a point."

"I don't know about that," Lucas teased, rubbing his jaw. "Beau said you've got a pretty mean right."

"Beau should have been sold to gypsies as an infant," she retorted. "I don't normally hit people. Beau is an exception because brute force is all he understands."

"I don't normally come on to women."

Marie's head shot up and she met those piercing eyes. "You don't look much like a monk," she observed.

The comment earned her a dazzling, spine-melting smile. "I said I didn't come on to women, not vice versa."

"That's really conceited," Marie said. "But I suppose there are a lot of women out there who are desperate to marry a doctor."

"Are you?"

"Not me," she said earnestly.

"Not husband shopping?"

She held his gaze. "Not when I could go to jail for the rest of my life."

Lucas's expression turned somber. "When I look at you, I forget that you're going through a real rough stretch."

"That's one way to put it. You aren't making things a whole lot easier."

"I guess my timing is a little off."

Marie reached out and touched his sleeve. "That wasn't a criticism, I was trying to be honest."

His fingers closed over her hand. "So was I."

"But your honesty is moving a little too fast for me."

One of his brows arched upward. "I thought you were the kind of person who acted spontaneously."

"I'm trying to break that habit. I'm not saying never, Lucas. I'm just asking you to let me concentrate on proving my innocence right now."

"Do I have a choice?"

"Please?"

"No promises. I've never tried to rein my feelings in before."

"You and Beau."

"What is that supposed to mean?" he asked, genuine concern in his voice.

"My brother doesn't exactly exercise restraint when it comes to women."

"Hang on," Lucas said. "I don't think we're communicating on the same plane here. Before you have me in the sack with every woman around, don't you think we should get to know each other first?"

Marie felt her cheeks flush. She didn't want to think of him in the sack—under any circumstances. "I guess so," she said quickly, before leaving the bedroom. She knew Lucas was behind her; the floor creaked beneath his weight.

"Since someone hit you, don't you think we should call the cops?"

"No."

"But—"

"I said no."

"Then let me check you out."

She stopped in her tracks. Keeping her back to him, she said, "Please don't be so nice to me."

"Why not? Most people think I'm a pretty nice guy."

"I know, I got the full report at the courthouse. You have your own groupies," she teased.

She felt him come closer. Close enough that his thighs brushed against her; close enough that she could feel the warmth of his breath in her hair. "Want to be my chief groupie?"

"You had me arrested," she said, but the statement lacked any real malice. In fact, she knew even before he voiced a denial that it wasn't his fault.

"I wish I could have refused to do Carl Lee's dirty work."

Marie swallowed. "Do you think I killed David?"

"I think it's highly improbable."

"Did you say that because you think that will make me jump into bed with you?"

"Ouch," he said with a chuckle. "You get right to the heart of the matter, don't you?"

"I don't believe in mincing words. It's a Delacroix trait."

His hands found her shoulders and he gently pulled her against him. Marie so wanted to close her eyes and simply enjoy the strength of his embrace. It would feel so good. It would be so easy. It would be insanity.

"Don't do this," she said.

"Do what?"

"Hold me. Comfort me. It can't lead to anything good."

"You won't know until you try."

"Really, Lucas..." She made a futile attempt to break free. "The only thing this will prove is that you're stronger than I am."

"You're wrong," he purred against her ear. "It has already proved that you feel as good as I thought you would. Underneath all that fabric is a very soft, very sensual woman."

Her knees felt like jelly. "Lucas, please?"

His mouth sought and found her ear. His breath came in warm waves as it washed over the skin that was exposed when he brushed her unruly hair to the side. He didn't actually kiss her. It was more like being branded by his lips as he tasted her earlobe, then her neck.

The deafening sound of her pulse pounded in her ears and she tried not to think about how very good this felt. Desiree was wrong. This man couldn't keep her safe from danger—he personified it!

"Really, Lucas," she said as she pulled free. She wasn't sure whether she was relieved or disappointed when he simply let her go. "I don't know why you would do something like that."

He shrugged. "The usual reasons."

"I hope, in the future, you'll refrain from that sort of thing."

Marie glanced up to find him smiling, his head tilted slightly to one side. "I don't like to plan for the future. I'm pretty spontaneous."

"Flirtatious," she corrected him. "Carl Lee said he would fire you if you didn't stay away from me."

"Carl Lee can go take a hike."

Marie let out an exasperated sigh. "We both know

he wasn't kidding. Carl Lee will fire you, and then where will you be?"

"I'm safe as far as my position at the hospital goes. Although Carl Lee is my boss, I'm protected by my contract at Lakeview. The only thing he can do is revoke my appointment as deputy coroner."

"I don't want to be responsible for that happening."

Lucas grew more serious. "Then you should understand how I feel, wondering whether I've helped build a case against an innocent person."

Marie searched his face. "What are you trying to say?"

"I'm just saying that your lack of a motive points me toward other possibilities."

"Does that mean you do or don't think I killed David?"

"The physical evidence is too pat. I'm not sure I can believe it."

"Do me a favor?"

Lucas nodded.

"Don't try to kiss me again until you've decided."

"I'M FINE," Marie insisted to her brother. "I put some ice on the swelling and I hardly even have a bump now." She had just been ready to walk out her apartment door when the phone rang, and it was too early in the morning to be anyone but family. Now she began to regret having answered the call.

"Why didn't Henderson take you to the hospital?" Beau demanded.

"It was my decision," Marie said. "And since he

obviously told you what happened, why didn't you ask him? I've got to go, Beau."

"Go where?"

"Out," Marie said, exasperated. "I love you. Bye."

"Marie!" she heard Beau yell just before she gently placed the receiver back in its cradle.

Using several hairpins, Marie piled her curly black hair on top of her head. She wasn't fond of leaving it loose, but her head was a little too tender for a scarf. "Maybe it will hold for a few hours," she told her reflection as she slipped a dozen silver bracelets onto her wrist.

Without a car at her disposal, she was forced to use public transportation to get to David's office. Even though the building was relatively close, the bus ride took thirty-five minutes and two transfers before she reached her destination. As she stepped down onto the sidewalk, she turned in time to catch a glimpse of the car immediately behind the bus. She wasn't certain, but she could have sworn she saw the redhead who had been in the back of the courtroom during her arraignment. Shading her eyes from the early morning sun, she read and repeated the license number until she found a pen and a slip of paper in her purse. After jotting down the number, she remained on the sidewalk, wondering if the woman could be following her.

Marie felt her anxiety build, and she glanced nervously up and down the deserted street. "What am I going to do if she comes back?" she whispered. "What if she was the one who hit me last night?" *What if my imagination is getting the better of me?*

she thought, and with a determined step, she hurried across the street and into the nondescript office complex.

Marie was relieved to find the front doors unlocked. Glancing around one last time, she slipped unnoticed inside the building. Passing the directory and the elevators, she opted for the stairway, just in case anyone was on the sixth floor at this ridiculous time of the morning. She checked her watch, slightly worried that so much of her window of opportunity had been eaten up by the bus trip.

Her calves were sore by the time she reached her destination. Carefully, she peeked through the window of the stairwell door, breathing normally when she saw the corridor empty. As quietly as possible, she found David's office and tried the door. It was locked. She pulled the shiny silver tools from her purse. Thanks to her sister Charly, Marie was well versed in the art of picking locks. As the youngest child, Charly had mastered lock picking as a means to get into the rooms and diaries of her older siblings. Luckily she'd redirected her talents and had just become a member of the police force in nearby Slidell.

Marie smiled when she heard the telltale metallic click of the tumblers. Slowly, she eased open the door and stepped into the darkened room.

Just then a hand clamped over her mouth.

CHAPTER SEVEN

MARIE LIFTED HER FOOT and brought it crashing down on the instep of her attacker. His viselike grip loosened just enough for her to swing an elbow into his midsection.

His groan came out on the rush of breath forced out by her defensive move. Marie scrambled free and headed for the door just as a pained voice demanded, "Are you trying to kill me?"

"Lucas?"

"I was a minute ago, now I'm not so sure."

"Oh, gosh," Marie said. She stumbled to a desk and managed to turn on a small lamp. "Are you okay?"

"Dandy." Lucas was hopping up and down, holding his foot in one hand and rubbing his stomach with the other. "Are you always so aggressive?"

"I thought you were the same guy who came after me last night," she wailed. "What *are* you doing here, anyway?"

"I was waiting for you. I guessed you'd make this your next stop."

"How did you get in?"

Lucas straightened, testing his foot in the process. "There was a set of keys with David's personal effects. How did you get in?"

"I picked the lock."

He gave her a sidelong glance. "You do have some interesting talents. At least now I understand how you got into David's apartment last night. How's the head?"

"I'm fine. I'm sorry I hit you."

Lucas smiled. "Me, too."

Marie found his good humor infectious and couldn't help smiling back. It was so easy being with Lucas.

"What are we looking for?" he asked.

"Since I don't have any enemies, I can only assume that David had at least one."

Lucas frowned. "David wasn't the kind of guy to make enemies. He was a psychiatrist, a therapist. He made his living resolving people's conflicts."

"I guess that's why the cops didn't take all his personal stuff into custody."

Marie frowned with disgust. "Why would they? He died at my shop. Once you found the poison in my jojoba oil, they probably didn't expend much effort looking at other possibilities."

He met her eyes. "Maybe they didn't take this stuff because there's nothing here of value. Ever think of that?"

"I still have to look," Marie insisted. "There was something in the notebook I saw in his apartment that struck me as odd."

"What was it?"

"It had to do with his schedule."

"Could you be more specific?" Lucas asked as he sat at the reception desk and opened the appointment book.

"I was knocked on the head before my brain could process what it was that bothered me. I tried brewing some memory-enhancing tea this morning, but it didn't help."

Standing behind him, Marie read over his shoulder as he flipped through the first few months of the year. Absently, she placed her hands on his shoulders and leaned even closer. Some of the entries were difficult to read.

"Marie?"

"Shush, I have to concentrate." She finished with the month of March and moved into April, then May.

"Marie?"

"I'm trying to concentrate."

"So am I, and I can't do it with your incredible body pressed against my back."

"Sorry," she yelped, jumping back. "I wasn't thinking."

"Neither can I when you're that close."

Her cheeks flaming hot, Marie silently berated herself for being so stupid. "Can we please stay focused on the task at hand?"

"I'm focused," Lucas said with a lecherous grin. "I'll even pretend to read the entries."

"Go into David's office and check things out in there."

"If I tell you you have a beautiful body, will you hold it against me?"

"Will you take your bad old jokes and get busy? We don't have a lot of time before people start coming in to work."

"I think I liked you better when you were kicking my butt."

"If you don't get busy, that's exactly what I'll do."

"An aggressive woman is *really* sexy."

"Henderson..." she warned.

Lucas raised his hands in surrender. "I'm going."

Marie read the entries for the first week of May for at least the third time.

Really sexy.

She read them a fourth time.

Really sexy.

"Blast!" she muttered, banishing his words from her brain. She lifted her head and found him in the next office, trying keys in the lock of the file cabinet. Each movement of his arms outlined his sinewy torso. It didn't take a whole lot of imagination to know he would look positively glorious without his shirt. She had felt the corded strength of his stomach with her elbow. She had only to close her eyes and she could imagine—

"Did David ever talk to you about Haven Cottages?"

Marie didn't meet his eyes, she was too afraid they might reveal her thoughts. "He and a partner held week-long intensive counseling sessions there. I think it was some sort of marriage-encounter thing. Why?"

"He sold his interest in Haven Cottages the day before he died."

"Is that unusual?"

"I found some old tax forms and it looks like the place was the next best thing to printing your own money."

"David was troubled by something recently. Maybe he wasn't interested in the hassle of running the place anymore."

"Maybe," Lucas said as he continued to pore through the documents.

"I think I know why he sold out," Marie said.

"Why?"

"Beginning in May, David was spending every other week up at Haven. Spending two weeks out of every month on the road gets old fast."

"How much does a week there run?"

Marie got up from the desk to pluck a brochure from a stand in the reception area. "Twenty-five hundred for basic counseling."

Lucas whistled. "I think David was underestimating his taxes. The financial records only report one week a month up at Haven."

Marie felt excitement course through her as she placed the pamphlet on David's desk. "Maybe someone knew what David was doing and was blackmailing him."

"Maybe I can find some of his bank records."

"I'll help," Marie said, joining him by the file cabinets. After a ten-minute search she found a neatly arranged file folder in the last cabinet. "Here it is!"

Lucas scanned the pages in the file, the frown lines on his forehead growing deeper by the minute. "This doesn't make any sense."

"What doesn't?"

"If David was being blackmailed, his accounts sure don't show it."

"Are you positive?"

"Absolutely," Lucas said, laying a few of the statements on the desk. "If anything, David was improving his cash flow. Looking at these, I would guess that he was converting all his investments into cash.''

''Is that normal?''

''Not really. He sold his interest in Haven. He sold off his entire investment portfolio. He's got more money in his checking account than the FDIC will guarantee.''

''Isn't that risky?''

''It's right up there with stuffing your money under the mattress.''

''Why would he do something like that?''

Lucas shrugged. ''Maybe David thought the stock market was about to bottom out.''

''That would explain selling off the stocks, but it doesn't explain why he cashed everything else in,'' she said.

''I'll run this past a friend of mine who's a broker. Maybe she can find a logical reason for what he was doing.''

''Maybe we should—''

Marie fell silent as the door to the reception area began to open. Before she could think, Lucas had grabbed her and yanked her into a tiny coat closet.

They were crushed together in the dark, cramped space. It took several seconds for Marie's eyes to adjust. It took several more for her heart to stop racing.

She could hear footsteps just beyond the door. Holding her breath, she tried to shift herself so that she wasn't rammed into him, but it wasn't to be. Her hands were trapped between them, her fingers pressed against the rock-hard muscle of his chest. Her cheek rested against his shoulder and her legs entwined with his, making it almost impossible to tell where hers stopped and his began.

The footsteps came close to their hiding place. She could feel Lucas's heartbeat accelerate through the fabric of his shirt. It was growing warm in the close confines of the closet, and she felt the beginnings of a cramp in her calf. She wondered how Lucas could bear it.

The footsteps stopped right next to the closet door. Marie felt the trickle of perspiration between her breasts just before the door was yanked open.

"You!" Marie yelled as the woman's features came into focus.

The redhead screamed at the same time, then turned and raced from the offices. In their haste to pursue her, Lucas and Marie practically tumbled out onto the floor.

"Wait!" Marie cried, trying to disentangle her legs from his.

"Hurry! She'll get away!"

"Not very far," Marie argued as she was lifted off the floor and set firmly on her feet. "I have her license plate number."

Lucas was obviously skeptical. "Desiree saw it in a vision?"

"Something like that."

"I'm not as trusting as you are. Stay put and I'll see if I can catch her."

"But—"

"Stay put! We don't know if she's armed or not."

Marie stopped trying to argue with him. If he wanted to race down six flights of stairs, he was welcome to it. She spent her time collecting the financial records and going through the appointment book.

Lucas returned ten minutes later, sweaty, winded and defeated.

"Did you have a good workout?"

"Great cardiovascular exercise."

"But unnecessary," Marie said.

"I got a decent look at her. I think I've seen her before."

"You have."

"What are you talking about?"

"She was at my arraignment."

"She was?"

"I think she's some sort of reporter."

"You think she came up here looking for a story?"

"Maybe."

"Is she following you?"

"I've seen her a couple of times in passing."

"Is there any chance she was the one who hit you last night?"

Marie thought for a minute before answering, "I don't think so. Didn't you see her face when she opened the closet door? She was more afraid than we were."

"You have a point there."

"I also have her plate number. I'm sure my sister can run a check on it as a favor."

"Shelby?"

"Charly—Charlotte. Didn't Beau tell you? She's a cop over in Slidell."

"Yes, he did. I must say, the Delacroix women are certainly a diverse group." His smile reached his eyes. "Come here, I have something I want to tell you."

"What?" she asked with apprehension.

Lucas held out his hand. "Please?"

He slipped one arm around her waist and drew her to him. Taking the pages from her, he placed them on the desk behind him.

To compensate for the marked difference in their heights, Lucas perched on the edge of the desk and pulled her into the cradle of his thighs. His eyes fell to her lips, and that simple action felt more intimate than any kiss. His free hand took a slow trip up her arm, over her shoulder, until finally his fingers tangled in the mass of hair, scattering the pins.

"I don't think this is such a swift idea," Marie confessed. "We are here illegally and it's getting close to eight. People are going to start showing up for work."

"Relax," he said sternly, and brought his mouth closer to hers. Marie felt every word as a puff of warm breath against her lips. "I'm simply following your instructions."

"My instructions?"

His nod was barely perceptible. "You said I couldn't kiss you until I believed in you." Each word was punctuated by a teasing brush of his lips against hers.

"You don't think I killed David?"

"I was never fully convinced, and after what happened to you last night, I'm even less convinced. David was my friend. Do you really think I'd be here with you if I thought you had killed him?"

"I don't know you, Lucas. This is all happening too fast. I just don't know...."

"Then I'll have to convince you," he whispered, and pulled her more intimately against him.

If Marie had had any doubts about his attraction to her, they were dispelled the instant she felt the strength of his desire. He pressed against her, igniting every erogenous zone in her body in a kind of flash fire she had never before experienced.

His mouth was magical, leaving burning kisses over her lips and face. She wouldn't have stopped him for the world. This was pure heaven. He seemed to know just when to apply pressure, just when to tease. Like some besotted damsel of days long past, Marie seemed helpless to do anything more energetic than cling to him in a type of heady desperation. Lucas had managed to bring her to a place she'd never been before, and with nothing more than a few kisses.

"Damn!" he muttered.

At first Marie wasn't sure why he had stopped. She just knew she didn't like it. It wasn't until he had pulled the beeper from his belt loop that the fog over her brain started to lift.

"I didn't think pathologists got emergency calls," she teased, impressed that she had managed to say the words in a relatively steady voice.

"I've never gotten an urgent page before, and I don't recognize the number."

He held it out to her and Marie stilled. "That's Beau's cell phone number. Why would he be paging you at this time of the morning?"

"Let's find out," Lucas suggested. He tested the

phone and, apparently finding it still connected, he dialed the number.

While he was waiting for someone to answer, he reached out and traced the side of her upturned face with his fingertip. Marie silently cursed her brother for his bad timing.

"This is Lucas, you paged me?"

The first thing she noticed was his hand stilling. Then she saw the flush of passion, along with all the other color, drain from his cheeks.

"What is it?"

He held up one finger to silence her. "I'll have her there in no time. Who is the attending surgeon?" There was a brief pause before he added, "He's a great neurosurgeon. You're in good hands."

"Is it Shelby?" Marie demanded, panic welling inside her. "Did the accident cause an aneurysm?"

Lucas gripped her shoulders and met her eyes. "It isn't Shelby," he said softly.

"Oh, God, it's Daddy, isn't it? Aunt Mary?" Marie felt desperate. "A neurosurgeon? Did Daddy have a stroke?"

"Listen," he urged in a soft, calming tone. "It isn't your father or your aunt."

"Uncle Philip? Grandfather?"

"Marie!" he said almost gruffly, giving her a gentle shake. "Your sister Charly was on patrol early this morning. She was trying to serve a warrant and—"

Marie backed away from him, clutching her throat with her hands. "Not Charly. She's only been a cop for four days."

Lucas pulled her into his arms as warm tears filled her eyes.

"She's been shot," he whispered as he stroked her back. "We need to get you to the hospital."

"Is she going to be okay?" Marie asked. "Of course she will," she answered, wiping the tears away with the back of her hand. "You hear about people being shot all the time and they recover. Charly is only twenty-five. She's really strong and—"

Lucas reached out and embraced her. "It's a head wound, Marie."

CHAPTER EIGHT

"HOW ARE YOU HOLDING UP?"

Marie raised her weary eyes to the kindly face of the elderly priest. "I'm doing okay, Uncle William. I'm just scared. She still hasn't come out of the coma, and the doctor said the bullet shattered her shoulder blade before it entered her head."

William placed his hand over hers. "Have faith."

"It's hard," she admitted. "I'd feel better if Daddy would go home and get some rest."

"Would you like me to speak to him?"

Marie sighed. "He might listen to you. He hasn't been home for three days."

Father William smiled down at her, his gentle eyes communicating the comfort and reassurance that came so naturally after a lifetime spent as a cleric.

"What about you?" he asked. "Have you left the hospital at all?"

Marie shook her head. "I just can't leave. I feel responsible."

"What on earth for?"

"I don't know. It seems as if my arrest has caused a downward spiral in this family. First Shelby and Joanna are run off the road, then Charly gets shot. You're lucky you weren't here a few hours ago. Uncle Philip and Grandfather nearly came to blows right here in the hospital.''

William didn't so much as flinch when she mentioned the warring factions. Probably because he knew better than most what his brothers were like. ''What started it this time?''

''Uncle Philip accused Grandfather of having some sort of curse put on him.''

''Oh dear, I hope you called security,'' William joked.

''Joanna took Uncle Philip home and Jax got custody of Grandfather.''

''How is your sister?''

''Jax is Jax. She's been a rock through all of this. She's been operating a shuttle back and forth to the hospital.''

Her father and Desiree emerged from the intensive care area where Charly was clinging to life with the aid of technology. Her father seemed to have aged ten years in three days. Marie rose and gave him a hug.

''Is there any change?'' she asked.

Justin shook his head. ''I can't stand much more of this.''

''Why don't you go home and take a rest?'' Marie pleaded. ''I promise I'll call you if anything happens.''

''She's right, Justin,'' William said. ''Let me take you home. You can't do Charly any good if you collapse from exhaustion.''

''I can't leave my baby like this,'' Justin insisted.

''She will heal,'' Desiree said with conviction.

For the first time, Marie doubted her mentor's predictions.

"The herbs will see to it."

"I'm praying," William said. "We all need to pray."

"But *you* need to rest," Marie insisted to her father. "Please let Uncle William take you home."

Justin rubbed his red eyes. "I don't know, Marie. What if she wakes up?"

"Not *if* she wakes up," Marie answered with a forced smile. *"When."*

Her father's shoulders slumped forward. "Maybe just long enough for a shower."

"I'll drive you," William said.

A few minutes later, Marie stood at the observation window, staring at her motionless younger sister. The clock on the wall indicated that it would be another twenty minutes before the nurses would permit her a fifteen-minute visit. The ICU at Lakeview Community had rather stringent policies regarding patient visitation.

Anxiety and caffeine from a zillion cups of coffee propelled her back down the corridor. Her legs felt like lead weights, and her heart was even heavier.

LUCAS WATCHED HER as she stared through the observation window, marveling that she was still standing. She had to be running on sheer determination and adrenaline. She turned and saw him, and Lucas felt his chest tighten when he noted the shimmer of unshed tears in her eyes.

"Hi."

"You should go home."

Marie shook her head. "I'm fine." Then her upturned face paled. "Has something happened?"

Quickly he shook his head. "No, I just came up to lend moral support and to see if I could talk you into taking a break."

Marie rubbed her bloodshot eyes. "I'm fine, really."

Lucas went to her, wrapping his arms around her. Marie seemed ready to collapse. "Mind if I keep you company for a while?"

"You don't need to do that," she argued without much enthusiasm. "It's got to be close to midnight. You'll probably want to get some sleep."

He led her to the soft sofa in the waiting room. "I'm the doctor—I'm the one who's supposed to give the orders."

"That's exactly the kind of attitude that turned me off traditional medicine."

"I don't follow you." He felt Marie relax somewhat as they sat together. Her head fell against his chest, and he gently massaged her tension-filled shoulders.

"Doctors are like dictators. They're demanding and arrogant and insensitive to their patients."

"My patients are dead," Lucas reminded her. Her weak laugh caused a tightness in his gut.

"You don't respect me."

"Aren't you being a little premature?" he teased. "Aren't you supposed to accuse me of that *after* we make love?"

"I didn't mean it like that. I've had a lot of time to think during all this."

"That sounds dangerous."

"You think aromatherapy is a big joke, don't you?"

Lucas placed a kiss on her brow. "I'll plead the fifth."

"Great. How do you expect us to have a meaningful conversation if you won't answer my questions?"

"Is this really important to you?"

He heard her sigh. "Yes. No. I don't know. My brain's not working right now. I guess I started thinking about it when my father fell apart earlier. He was ranting and raving that he should have never permitted Charly to go into law enforcement. As if he could have stopped her."

"Did they argue about it?"

"All the time. I think those arguments are haunting him now."

"Your father doesn't impress me as a tormented man."

"His ghosts are private. Most of them came with his divorce from my mother."

"Is that why you're so intent on going slowly with me?"

Marie shifted and glanced up at him. "No. I just don't want to start something I could only finish on visiting days."

"That's good to know," he said, cradling her back against his chest. "A lot of children carry the scars of their parents' divorce into adulthood."

"That would be Beau, though he'd chew off his tongue before he'd admit it to anyone."

"Was it rough?"

"The divorce was easy. It was what came afterward that made me crazy."

"What was that?"

Marie laughed softly. "Did you ever see that movie

with Bing Crosby and Grace Kelly? *The Country Girl?*''

Lucas nodded.

''At some point during the film, Bing Crosby's character says something like, 'The only thing more obvious than two people looking longingly at each other is two people trying not to.' That pretty much sums up the relationship between my parents since they split up.''

Marie settled against him, her palms resting on his chest. He fell silent, hoping she might relax enough to get a few minutes of much needed rest. The elevator door opened and a lab technician came down the hallway. Absently, Lucas noted that the guy was wearing a baseball cap without a paper sleeve on it. He made a mental note to speak to the fellow's supervisor. He also didn't have shoe covers on his feet. If Marie hadn't been asleep on his shoulder, he would have taken the guy to task then and there. The technician wasn't exempt from hospital policy just because he worked the midnight shift.

And he worked quickly, Lucas noted as he watched the man leave Charly's room. He hadn't been in there more than a few minutes.

Marie's hair smelled of flowers and felt like silk between his fingers. *Respect.* The memory of her question caused him to frown. Of course he respected her. She was intelligent, beautiful, an entrepreneur. What wouldn't he respect?

He didn't get a chance to answer his own question. The alarm at the nurse's station alerted him instantly.

''What is it?'' Marie asked, bolting upright.

''Wait here!'' Lucas said. He jogged over to the

window. After a quick assessment, he grabbed a gown and gloves from a nearby cart and shrugged into them.

"Lucas!" Marie called. "Tell me what's happening."

"She's coding."

Pushing the image of her tortured features from his mind, he went into the room.

"What the hell is going on?" he growled.

"Respiration is zero," the nurse told him. "Heartbeat is erratic, skin is clammy."

Lucas bent to examine Charly and noted the red blotches on her face. He swore. "Pull everything but the saline and get me some glucose. Now!"

"I'll page Dr. Greenbaum," she said as she handed him a syringe.

"You can page every doctor on the service as soon as you hang a glucose drip."

It had been quite a number of years since Lucas had practiced emergency medicine, and he could only hope that his diagnosis was correct. With only a brief hesitation, he stuck the needle into the open IV line and fed the medicine into Charly's body.

Within seconds, her respiration began to stabilize.

"Nice work, Dr. Henderson," the nurse said through tight lips. "I'll go and page her physician now, if that's all right with you?"

"She'll need a blood sugar screen and I want a full explanation."

"What?"

"I don't think she developed diabetes from a gunshot wound. Someone screwed up her meds."

The nurse shrank back as if he'd slapped her. "Is that all?"

"For now."

Lucas stayed at her bedside for several minutes, needing to make sure that she was over the crisis. When he was sure that her condition was stable, he went to get Marie.

"Is she dead?" Marie asked, tears spilling down her cheeks.

Lucas drew her to him. "Nope. Your sister is a fighter."

"What were you doing in there for so long?"

Lucas didn't think it would be a good idea to tell her that his hospital had been negligent to the point of a near fatality, so he simply asked, "Would you like to see her?"

"Please."

Marie walked around to the opposite side of the bed. Out of habit, Lucas plucked the metal chart from the foot of the bed. He started when the cardiac monitor signaled a sudden change in rhythm. Not again, he groaned silently, then yanked open the door and yelled "Nurse!"

"What is it?" Marie asked in a panicked voice.

Lucas raised his hand as he continued to watch the monitor. "Talk to her," he told Marie.

"Talk about what?"

"Anything."

"Charly, please wake up."

The monitor kept moving in an erratic fashion.

"I think I felt her hand move," Marie gasped. "Charly? C'mon Charly, please? Charly, do you know you have a dress on!"

Lucas watched the woman in the bed. A wad of gauze covered her head and the skin around her eyes was blackened from surgery. Suddenly her eyelids started to twitch.

"Look!" Marie cried. "She's trying to open her eyes!"

"You'd better get her doctor up here," Lucas told the nurse. "I'll start manual stimulation." He threw the sheet back, exposing Charly's feet. Pulling a pen from his coat, he began running the sharp edge of the cap along the sensitive area of her instep. He almost cheered when she responded. "Talk to her, Marie. Yell if you have to."

"Charly!" Marie shouted.

The bed was suddenly surrounded with an assortment of medical personnel. Lucas relinquished his position when the attending neurosurgeon appeared. He went to stand next to Marie, completely caught up in the type of drama he hadn't experienced since the long-ago days of his residency.

His colleagues worked for the better part of an hour before Charly's eyes finally fluttered open. Marie started to cry, then turned and gave him an unexpected but much appreciated hug. "Thank you," she murmured against his shirt.

"I didn't do anything."

Charly did the expected and tried to yank the oxygen tubing off her face. She moved her bandaged head in the direction of Marie's voice. "Am I really wearing a dress?" she asked in a weak voice.

Marie laughed, as did everyone else in the room. Relief was palpable. "It's more like a nightgown," Marie explained.

"Who was the man?" Charly asked.

"That's Dr. Henderson," the nurse supplied. "And now we've got to get this mask back in place."

Charly protested weakly as the nurse placed the oxygen mask over her face once more.

Marie was deliriously happy until the doctor told them to clear the room. She squeezed her sister's hand and promised she'd be back as soon as she could.

"THIS REALLY ISN'T necessary," Marie said much later as she slipped into the passenger side of Lucas's car.

"I want to make sure that you get home and get some sleep."

Marie didn't feel tired anymore. In fact, she felt exhilarated by Charly's recovery. In less than two hours, Charly had passed all the preliminary tests with flying colors. Even the unemotional neurosurgeon was predicting a full recovery. "I don't think I want to go to sleep now."

"You'll be out the minute your head hits the pillow," Lucas promised her. "I'm a doctor. I know about these things."

"I really can't thank you enough," Marie said. "I don't know what you did to get her to wake up, but—"

"It wasn't me," he assured her. "If I had to guess, I'd say it was that bit you said to her about the dress that did it. Care to explain?"

"Charly hates wearing dresses. She thinks being a woman is a weakness."

"But what about her sisters? You all grew up in the same house, right?"

"Charly has this silly notion that she can't compete with the rest of the Delacroix girls," Marie answered. She settled back against the leather seat, enjoying the feel of the crisp night air on her face. Lucas drove with the convertible top down, and the cool breeze was like a tonic after the stale hospital air. "She decided she'd have better odds competing with the Delacroix men."

"Charly's wrong. She's an attractive woman— even beneath all those bandages. Of course, she's not a pretty as you are," he added quickly.

Marie laughed. "Nice save, Lucas. But you're right. Unfortunately, Charly had a bad experience in college and won't let a man get within ten feet of her unless it's to shag fly balls."

"How bad?"

The affront she heard in those words made her smile. "It isn't what you're thinking. It actually happened to her roommate. No wonder Beau likes you. He had the same reaction when I mentioned it to him. He was ready to ride off on his trusty steed to avenge her honor until I explained things."

He glanced over long enough to give her a wink. "My steed is at your service, madam."

Holding her hair in one hand, she lifted her face to the starry sky. "It's a beautiful night."

"The night isn't the only thing that's beautiful."

Marie turned and their eyes met once more. Something had changed in the terrible hours when Charly had battled for survival. Marie now looked at the man seated so close to her in a whole new light. It was hard to think back to a time when Lucas hadn't been there for support. He'd spent every spare moment by her side. He'd held her when she cried, listened as she'd rambled on about her childhood. Tentatively, she slid her hand across the console until it rested on his. "I don't think I could have gotten through this without you."

"Sure you could. But I'm glad I was around to help."

"You really have helped," she said. "I don't know how I'll ever be able to thank you."

Lucas stopped for a traffic light and turned to her. "There is one thing you could do for me."

"Anything."

"Marry me."

CHAPTER NINE

"AND I WAS AFRAID it was Charly who would be brain damaged," Marie said as she pushed open the door to her apartment. "Obviously I should have been concerned about you."

"Will you please shut up and let me explain?"

"Explain what, Lucas?" Marie went to the cupboard took out some herbal tea, then put the kettle on to boil.

He came into the kitchen wearing a very determined and frustrated expression. In fact, his eyes were so intense that Marie actually retreated. She didn't stop until she felt the cool surface of the refrigerator at her back. Instinctively she reached up, planting her palms against his massive chest.

Lucas placed one hand on either side of her head. Then, with absolutely no effort, he simply leaned his big body into her. She didn't dare move.

"I'm not real big on brute strength," she informed him.

"At least I finally got your attention," he said in a much less threatening tone.

"You certainly got my attention in the car. I'm simply going to attribute your proposal to a slight lapse of sanity on your part."

"Marie, calm down and hear me out. That's all I ask."

Marie struggled briefly, then gave up in quiet frustration. Her anger slowly subsided. She knew Lucas well enough to realize that he simply hadn't been toying with her emotions when he'd made his ridiculous proposal. "So, talk."

"I've narrowed the search down to Haven."

It took her brain a minute to switch gears. "You think someone at Haven was blackmailing David?"

"Possibly."

"So, we'll go up and interview—"

"I've tried that."

"You went up there?"

He shook his head. The action caused his body to move ever so slightly. But it was just enough to remind Marie of their closeness. She bit down on her bottom lip to keep from begging to be released. The sooner he finished, the sooner he would let her go.

"I've called. Haven prides itself on discretion. No interviews. No tours. The only way in is as a married couple."

"That's why you asked me to marry you?"

There was a flicker of emotion in his eyes that she didn't know how to read, but all he said was, "I can't think of any other reason, can you?"

"We'll just tell them we're married," she suggested.

"We'd be required to produce a certificate in order to register."

"We'll forge one. I'm sure someone in my family can—"

"They're real sticklers at Haven," he explained. "Apparently they verify everything."

The struggle went out of her as she considered the possibility. "You would actually marry me just to get into Haven?"

"No. I'd marry you to find David's killer." His expression grew determined. "And to clear your name."

"A CHRISTMAS EVE WEDDING." Beau sighed. "How romantic."

"Be quiet," Marie snapped. Her nerves were frazzled beyond hope.

"Calm down. You're marrying Lucas, not a serial killer."

She glared at him. "You're my big brother. Why don't you talk me out of this?"

"Not on your life. Lucas is bigger than I am."

Marie checked her reflection in the mirror. Then she frowned. "I look like I'm going to an afternoon tea."

Beau reached out and took her hand, twirling her so that the yards of fabric billowed out from her calves. "You aren't upset over your clothes," he said pointedly. "I'll come through for you, if that's what you want. I can intercept Lucas at the courthouse and tell him you've changed your mind."

"I can't change my mind," she grumbled. "I lost it a week ago when I agreed to this plan."

Beau laughed. "Your instincts told you to accept. It seems to me that you've done pretty well by following your gut so far."

She smiled at him. "Do you respect me?"

"Of course not."

She gave him a playful slap. "Be serious, Beau. Do you think what I do is silly—the aromatherapy, I mean?"

"No. Why?"

"Lucas does."

"Did he say that?"

Marie shrugged and turned back to the mirror. She arranged her hair on top of her head while she contemplated her answer. "He hasn't actually said it, but I know that's how he feels."

"I thought Desiree had a lock on reading minds."

"I don't have to read his mind to know that he doesn't think very much of what I do. And what I do is who I am."

Beau came up behind her and placed his hands on her shoulders. Their eyes met in the reflection. "Think on that some more, Marie. And don't sell Lucas short, he's a good man."

"He'll be a dead man when Daddy finds out what I've done."

"Forget the old man. I'll handle the family," Beau reassured her. "Though I still haven't come up with a good explanation for why you're going to miss Christmas dinner at Aunt Mary's."

Marie bent her head to brush her cheek against his hand. "What would we do without you to keep us all out of trouble?"

"I think Henderson will be trouble, Marie."

"What is that supposed to mean?"

Beau shrugged and turned away from her. "It's always been important for you to be independent. Somewhere along the line, you've confused being independent with being alone. Lucas doesn't impress me as the kind of man who would want his wife to be a doormat.''

''You're making it sound like we're doing happily-ever-after here. Lucas and I have agreed to a quiet divorce after the trial.''

''You both agreed?'' Beau challenged. ''Or you decreed?''

''TELL ME AGAIN why I'm going to allow you to marry my kid sister,'' Beau said as they stood together in one of the anterooms of the courthouse.

''Everything will work out in time,'' Lucas insisted.

''I get the feeling that there's something you aren't telling me.''

''What's there to tell? Marie and I are getting married.''

''Marie doesn't get married at the drop of a hat. Marie doesn't even go on a date unless the moon and the planets are in the correct alignment.''

Lucas smiled as he tugged at his tie. ''Our marriage might be the only thing that keeps her out of jail.''

''You two aren't fooling anyone, except maybe yourselves. And if you expect me to stand up for you as your best man, Lucas, I think you ought to level with me.''

''I have,'' he answered. ''I asked Marie to marry me. She accepted.''

''There's more to this than just the trial, right?''

Lucas made a noncommittal sound. ''Marrying Marie is an expedient way to get into Haven. Nothing more.''

"At the risk of sounding corny, what exactly are your intentions?"

"To get married."

"For how long?"

"I don't know."

Marie walked into the room just then. Her appearance was enough to render him deaf and mute. The gauzy white dress floated around her dainty ankles, a stark contrast to her exotic darkness. The woman was truly a vision. A very nervous vision, if her shaky hands were any indication.

"Last chance to run," Beau whispered.

"I'm not running, Beau. Lucas and I both know what we're getting into."

"I doubt that," Beau muttered. "Shall we? Judge Calloway is waiting."

Lucas wasn't sure what he had expected, but it wasn't this woman frozen with fear. At least he hoped it was fear. Throughout the brief ceremony he actually held his breath until she had uttered her vows.

"Do you have a ring?" the judge asked.

Lucas took her left hand and slipped the band on her finger. Her hands were like ice and her lashes hid her eyes. The only response that hadn't been part of the civil ceremony was her little gasp of surprise when he placed the ring on her finger. That made him feel a bit more secure. The band of diamonds had been a hurried purchase, and he wasn't sure unconventional Marie would like it. He still wasn't sure, since he couldn't see her eyes, but the judge was coming to his rescue.

"You may kiss the bride."

Lucas waited, knowing full well he would kiss her.

He wanted her to look at him when he did. Marie's lashes fluttered, then lifted as their eyes met. Time was suspended as he gazed into her eyes, satisfied when he saw the spark of desire turn the gray to silver. He yearned for the feel of her mouth under his, would have devoured her if the circumstances had been different. He wanted, no, needed her to know that. Placing the soft brush of a kiss against her lips was the purest form of torture. But it was enough. For now.

"WHERE ARE WE GOING?"

"My place," Lucas answered. So she was finally talking. "I have a condo near the hospital. I've gotten together David's personal effects, the appointment book we took from his office and your client records. I thought we could look for some connection."

"Oh."

Lucas fought the urge to chuckle. "Was there something else you wanted to do tonight?" He was damn impressed that his voice sounded so casual.

"Not me," she breathed, fairly jumping out of his car.

He followed her out of the car and into his building. Once they were in the elevator, Lucas bent his head and gave her a gentle kiss, designed to entice. With utmost care, he held her face in his palms. It was an honest move on his part, and he took heart that Marie didn't turn away.

When the elevator stopped, he lifted her into his arms and carried her to the door.

"This is silly," she said on a giggle.

The sound of her laughter made him want to pound

on his chest. She was enjoying this. She had to feel something for him. And if she did, Lucas knew he had at least a fighting chance.

"You can put me down now," Marie said as he walked into the condo, flipping light switches with his elbow. "Really, Lucas. You'll strain something."

"I hardly think so. I've carried tissue samples that weigh more than you do."

"Such flattery."

He kissed her as he gently lowered her to the floor. He wanted to toss her down onto the pillows in front of the fireplace and make love to her. He wondered how long he could wait. Especially when he felt her melt against him as his tongue moistened her lower lip.

He allowed his hands to explore the outline of her rib cage. The thin fabric of her dress left little to his imagination. Judging by the way the material moved, he knew her skin would be as soft as silk. If only he could get to it.

The pillows and the fireplace were too far away, so he worked his way down her body. Cradling her body against his, he rolled onto his back, never breaking the seal of their lips.

He was burning up. She felt so good. His fingers groped at the pins holding her hair until it was finally loose. He could just imagine how she would look in his bed with all that black hair framing her face. He felt the groan in his throat. Then he felt the first tentative touches as the tips of her fingernails etched a path along his jawline. She touched his hair, his face, then kneaded his shoulders. He was going to explode.

"Wait," she breathed, placing her hands on the

floor and bracing her elbows so that her sweet mouth was out of his reach. "Lucas..."

Lucas allowed his arms to fall to the floor with a thud. He knew enough about women to know when one was about to put on the brakes. Marie's were screeching to a halt.

Scrambling, she got to her feet and adjusted her clothing. If it hadn't been for the wild disarray of her hair, he might have thought he had imagined the whole encounter.

"I should explain."

He put up his hand. "No explanation necessary.

"But—"

"Really," Lucas cut in. He pulled himself into a sitting position, then stood. "Want a drink?"

"No."

He went to the bar and poured himself a rather generous brandy. Through the sliding glass doors, he could see the glittering lights of New Orleans. That was what had sold him on the condo in the first place. But he would have gladly traded the view for just five more minutes with Marie. *His wife.* He swallowed the amber liquid in one long drink.

He was pouring a refill when Marie finally spoke. "Can I take a tour?"

"Sure, but it isn't anything like Riverwood."

"Few places are," she agreed. "This is nice."

He shrugged. "C'mon, I'll show you around."

"You're being awfully civil," she commented as she followed him down the hallway.

"My mother taught me that no means no."

"Sounds like a smart lady."

"She was. This is the guest room, but I haven't gotten around to putting any furniture in it."

"Was?"

"My parents died in a hotel fire when I was in college."

"That's terrible."

"I still miss them, but if they had to die, at least they were together."

He stood in the hallway, and Marie leaned against the door of the guest room, staring up at him rather intently. "What is it?" he asked.

"I guess it just dawned on me that I really don't know very much about you."

"Ask questions. I'm big on honesty."

"What if I ask you something that you don't want to answer?"

Lucas took another sip of his drink. "I don't have too many secrets."

He was glad to note that she seemed pleased by his answer. Especially since it was killing him to engage in idle chitchat when he had other, more interesting things on his mind. "This is the bedroom. There's a bathroom through there and another one off the den on the other side of the living room."

Marie seemed to relax as the evening wore on. Surprisingly, Lucas discovered that he was actually enjoying himself. It had been a long time since he'd spent an evening at home doing nothing. He also discovered that Marie was a great cook. She even managed to make a decent meal out of the spare offerings he kept on hand. He lit a fire and tuned the stereo to a station playing Christmas carols.

"You don't have a tree," she said, kicking off her

shoes. She snuggled against one of the pillows near the fire.

Lucas was lying on the floor with his feet crossed at the ankles and his head resting against the sofa. He watched as the firelight reflected in her eyes and off her hair. He was sure she had no idea how sexy she looked at that moment.

"Is there a reason?"

"For what?" he asked.

"Why you don't have a tree."

"Laziness," he admitted sheepishly. "I can probably go out and find one now if you'd—"

"It wasn't a criticism," Marie insisted. "I guess I was just trying to make conversation."

"Are you one of those people who can't stand long silences?"

She shrugged and gave him a smile. "Large-family syndrome."

"Only-child syndrome."

"Were you lonely?"

"Heck, no," Lucas told her. "I didn't have to share."

Marie tossed her head back and filled his modest home with laughter. It seemed right. *Too right.*

Lucas swirled his brandy and kept his eyes downcast as he asked, "Is this so bad?"

"Your house? No, it's—"

"Not the house. This. Us."

Marie's expression slammed shut like a door. Quickly, she got to her feet and gathered together all the materials they had on David's life.

"This was a good idea," she began. "With only a matter of days before my trial—"

She fell silent the instant he went over and touched her arm. Her spine was stiff and he could almost hear her holding her breath. He'd pushed too hard, too fast. He wouldn't make that mistake again.

"I'm sorry about earlier," he said.

"I don't want to make a mistake that will affect both our lives."

"I'm not so sure it would be a mistake."

Marie took his hand and pressed it against her lips. "I seem to run out of willpower when you're around." Her eyes searched his face, then settled on his eyes. "There's so much we don't know about each other. There's no need to rush."

Speak for yourself. "I understand."

"Thanks. Now, let's get to work."

Work wasn't what he wanted, but it was all he got. Lucas took David's appointment book and they spent an hour trying to match the names to someone who had also been a client or customer at Marie's shop.

"I only had that bottle in the shop for a month," Marie explained. "If David's killer came in, it would have to have been a recent visit."

"Are these records complete?"

"Only the credit card purchases have names. I never bothered to put them on the cash receipts."

"How many did you have in the month of November?" Lucas asked as he flipped to that period in the appointment book.

"Over eighty."

Lucas whistled. "Could a customer have gone into the back room without your noticing?"

"Maybe," she said. "Definitely, if they happened

to come in when I was upstairs or across the street getting something to eat.''

He gaped at her. "You leave your shop unattended?"

Marie nodded. "The lady next door keeps an eye out."

"So pretty much anyone could just stroll in and plant a poison."

"You don't have to get testy," Marie snapped.

"That isn't a very smart way to run a business."

"Thanks for the condescension. I'll take anything from you but that." Tossing the receipts onto the table, Marie stomped into the bathroom and closed the door with a resounding thud.

"Well-done, you ass," Lucas muttered to himself, trying to plan his next move.

Since he didn't want to run the risk of disturbing her and since he heard the shower come on, he decided to give her a chance to cool off before he apologized. His wife sure had one hell of a temper.

Wife.

He smiled. Leaning back in the chair, Lucas hoisted his feet up onto the adjacent chair. He picked up David's wallet—the one he had promised to hand over to the cops more than a week ago—and turned it over in his hands. The soft leather was curved, indicating that David had kept it in his back pocket. He opened it and found the expected—several credit cards, a driver's license. He ran his finger over the photograph on the license, which was encased in clear plastic.

His fingertip detected a ridge, and he realized that the license was in a plastic case rather than laminated. As he pulled the license out, a small white rectangle fluttered to the floor. He retrieved it and carefully turned it over.

When Marie reappeared a short time later, Lucas was still seated in his chair.

"Lucas, I'm really sorry," she began.

The fact that she was wearing one of his shirts and looking more beautiful than ever didn't matter. She could have walked in buck naked and it wouldn't have mattered.

"I really thought you were innocent."

Marie looked confused. "What are you talking about? What do you have in your hand?"

"You can stop pretending, Marie. I'm your husband, so I can't be compelled to testify against you. You really suckered me. No motive, right?"

"You're scaring me, Lucas. Why are you so angry?"

"I'd like to wring your neck."

"Why?"

"Because of this!" he growled, thrusting the photograph toward her. "I believe that *is* you attached to David's lips. Were you sleeping with him right up to the time you killed him?"

CHAPTER TEN

"OPEN THE DOOR."

Marie began to pace. Two days hidden away in a hotel, far from her new husband, hadn't dimmed the memory of his cold eyes when he had discovered the photograph of her kissing David. She also hadn't forgotten that he had been unwilling to even listen to an explanation. That memory gave fortitude to her words as she called "Go to hell!" through the door.

"Marie! I'm getting mad!".

"I don't care," she called back.

She jumped when she felt the wood shudder as his shoulder must have crashed against it.

"We have to talk."

"We talked two days ago. You called me a killer."

"Marie," he said in a pleading tone. "Please open this door. I really don't want to break my shoulder just to have a conversation with my wife."

"I won't be your wife for long. Shelby is working on that as we speak."

"No, she isn't."

"What?" Marie demanded, opening the door as far as the safety chain would allow. "What have you done?"

Lucas looked tired and his chin was covered with

a two-day stubble. "Let me in. People are gaping at me. They'll probably call the cops soon."

Marie closed the door long enough to unfasten the chain, then she opened it and Lucas barreled in.

"How did you find me?"

"Beau."

"I knew I should have drowned him when we were children."

"I wouldn't have thought you were the type to run and hide."

She glared at the man. "And I would have thought you were the type who would have at least given me the opportunity to explain. I guess we were both wrong."

Lucas half sat, half fell onto the unmade bed. His head dropped into his hands. He didn't look like the ogre of her dreams at that instant. He looked tormented.

"I've been searching for you since you bolted from my place."

Marie leaned against the chipped dresser and crossed her arms over her chest. "You wasted your time."

He sighed heavily and lifted his head. "No, I acted like a possessive jerk. I don't know what came over me."

It would have been so much easier if he hadn't been looking at her with such sincerity in his eyes. It would have been easier still if he hadn't admitted to feeling possessive.

Lucas winced. "I'm really sorry I got so angry, but could you at least try to see past my poor behavior?

That picture was a huge shock to me. I had no idea that David was anything more than your client."

Marie's insides were churning. It was so tempting to give in to her strong desire to seek comfort in his arms. She was so confused! She took a breath and went to the window, toying with the edge of the drape. "David and I dated for a short time."

"Were you in love with him?"

Marie rubbed her eyes. Was that really torment she heard in his voice? Impossible. "No. Which is why I was so surprised by that photograph. I don't know why David would have kept that in his wallet all this time."

"Maybe David loved you."

Marie smiled and shook her head. "I doubt it. I think I would have known if he felt something more than friendship for me. Incidentally, that picture was taken on David's birthday by my brother. It was completely innocent."

Lucas stood and came over to her. Tentatively, he reached out and captured her chin, lifting her face to his. His eyes searched hers for a long, quiet moment before his attention dropped to her left hand. He gave a faint smile. "You didn't take off the ring. Is that a sign that you're willing to overlook my juvenile behavior?"

His hopeful grin chiseled away at her defenses. "I've never run from an argument before in my life. What is it about you that makes me act like this?"

"Maybe," he mused in a voice as smooth as liquid velvet, "you like me. It might surprise you to know that some women find me irresistible."

Marie silently admitted that she wasn't at all surprised. Not when he looked at her with such intensity. Not when she could feel the heat of his breath on her face. If only she hadn't spent her every waking hour thinking about him. If only the memory of his kiss hadn't haunted her dreams. "I'm not 'some women.'"

His expression grew solemn as his eyes met hers. "I'm just beginning to realize that." He gave her cheek a final, gentle stroke before his hand slipped away.

Her heart fluttered. She didn't dare open her mouth, certain that if she did, an invitation would come spilling forth.

"It's December 26. Do you know what that means?" he asked.

"After-Christmas sales?"

Lucas smiled. "Guess again."

"I'm out of guesses."

He reached into the breast pocket of his tweed jacket and produced a rumpled fax. He taunted her by holding it just above her reach. "We don't have a lot of time."

"For what."

"If we leave now, we can swing by your place, pack and be in Monroe by dinnertime."

"Why do we want to be there?"

"Because the Haven Cottages are expecting Dr. and Mrs. Henderson in the morning."

IT WAS UNUSUALLY CHILLY as they left New Orleans and drove over the Twin Span bridge. Marie's bracelets and earrings jingled in the cool breeze that blew off Lake Pontchartrain.

"I can put the top up," Lucas said.

"Don't bother. I'm fine."

"Take my jacket out of the back seat and put it around your shoulders."

"Thanks," she said, reaching back. The jacket smelled like Lucas. She warmed up in no time. "How are we going to explain a need for counseling when we've only been married two days?"

"I told them that we want to build a strong marriage, so we thought we could benefit from the program."

"And they bought that?"

Lucas shrugged. "The lady I spoke to thought it was a wonderful idea."

"That was probably after she ran a credit check on you."

Lucas laughed. "That's a pretty cynical attitude for a woman who sells herbs and scented candles."

"Please don't make fun of aromatherapy. Just because you don't understand something, doesn't mean—"

Lucas placed a finger against her lips. "I didn't mean it that way. How come Beau can tease you about your profession and I can't?"

Because Beau loves me. She was sure Lucas didn't take her seriously. He didn't respect her. That hurt.

"If I promise not to make any more aromatherapy jokes, will you stop pouting?"

"I never pout."

"Beau says you do. He told me you were the moody one in the group."

"Beau should have his tongue cut out."

"He's only doing what any big brother would do."

"How would you know? You're an only child."

Lucas gave her a teasing wink. "But I have come up against a few overprotective big brothers in my day."

"I'm not interested in hearing about your past conquests."

"Good, because I'd rather talk about what I found out about Haven Cottages."

"Me, too." Marie battled the unruly strands of hair being whipped out of her scarf by the wind. "How did you get any information? I thought they were a tight-lipped group."

"It helps to be a deputy coroner."

"You mean an ex-deputy coroner. I saw the interview with Carl Lee in this morning's paper. He was pretty decent about your part in all of this. At least he was kind enough not to try and convict me in the press."

"He was a little different when he talked to me," Lucas said. "But I didn't really like being a deputy coroner, anyway."

Marie felt guilt surround her like a cloak. "I'm so sorry that this has cost you—"

"Don't give it a thought. Remember, I'm still a staff pathologist at Lakeview. Anyway, I'm actually kind of relieved."

"Why?"

"Working for Carl Lee as a deputy coroner was getting a little too political for my blood."

"If you don't like politics, you shouldn't have married a Delacroix. If my father heard you say that, he'd probably disown us both."

"Your father is a federal judge, right?"

"Until his daughter gets convicted and they impeach him."

Lucas reached over and gave her leg a squeeze. "I got you into this mess. I'll get you out."

And then what? Her solitary time in the hotel had left her plagued with conflicting feelings and more than just a few questions. The most important one being why? Why was a virtual stranger—an incredibly gorgeous stranger—going to such lengths to help her? It didn't make sense. Nothing in her life was making much sense.

Deal with that later, she admonished herself. *Focus on clearing your name.* "Tell me about Haven."

"Haven Cottages Corporation was started five years ago by David and his partner, Graham Nash. Equal shares of privately held stock."

"Do you know anything about Nash?"

"No."

"I met him once," Marie said. "It was at one of the functions I went to with David. He was rather insistent I accompany him to a lot of professional events."

"If you and David weren't...serious, was it possible that he was using you?"

"For what?" Marie asked. "David was fun to be with and completely nonthreatening."

Lucas gave her a quick glance. "He never tried to...?"

"Never," Marie insisted, thinking back on those dates. "He knew I was lonely. I just assumed that he took me to places because he was trying to be sweet and he preferred to have an escort."

"That doesn't sound like the David I knew."

"What does that mean?"

"In college, David had quite a reputation with women. And it wasn't for being sweet."

Marie sighed. "Maybe I just wasn't his type."

"Or maybe there was something else to it."

"Like what?"

"I don't know yet. For now, let's concentrate on what we do know. What did you think when you met Graham?"

"He was nice—pensive, pretty much a typical psychiatrist. I had the impression that he would love nothing better than to show me inkblots."

Lucas laughed. "Marie, any man who would want to show you inkblots should have his head examined."

She frowned. "It might surprise you to know that some people think I'm intelligent. Some people—"

Lucas silenced her when he placed his hand on her thigh and gave another squeeze. "I was implying that any man who could spend time with you and think of anything other than making love to you is and was a fool."

"Oh," Marie breathed. Her entire body tingled as his words reverberated in her brain. Then suddenly his words were replaced by a vivid mental picture of what it might be like to make love with Lucas. Her face flushed hotly as she chased the errant thoughts from her brain. She had to concentrate on clearing her name, not give in to adolescent fantasies. "You know, now that you mention it, there *was* something strange about those dates with David."

"Tell me about them."

"We went out to dinner a lot—often to work-related events. I especially remember a picnic last spring. It was a bunch of couples from Haven Cottages. Some kind of reunion thing. That's when I met Graham—only briefly.''

''What was strange about the picnic?''

Marie thought for a minute before answering. ''It wasn't the picnic, it was David.''

''What about David?'' Lucas asked excitedly.

''David always treated me like a sister.''

''Are we talking about the same David Markum?''

''Do you want me to tell you this or not?''

Lucas's only response was a slow, circular movement of the hand that rested on her thigh. Marie wasn't sure she could speak, let alone make sense, while he touched her. ''Sometimes David would act weird. That's why I stopped agreeing to go out with him.''

''Weird how?''

''Every now and then he would treat me like we were more than just friends.''

''*That's* the David I knew.''

''Lucas...'' she warned.

''Sorry, you were saying?''

''It isn't something I can explain. It's just that sometimes I had the feeling there was a specific reason why he wanted us to be seen together.''

''Maybe he was using you to make another woman jealous. Ever consider that?''

Marie nodded. ''I even asked him about it the night I told him I couldn't keep accompanying him to all those events.''

''And he said?''

"Nothing. He laughed and said I was imagining things. At the time, it made me feel like a real fool."

Lucas turned the car off the highway at the exit marked Monroe. He steered the convertible into a fairly decent-looking motel. It was a definite step up from the place where she had spent the past two nights hiding.

"How far is Haven from here?"

"About a thirty-minute drive." Lucas swung his own bag over his shoulder and carried Marie's in his hand. They found the office by following a blue line painted on the walkway. "My travel agent promised me it was clean," he whispered, holding the door open.

Marie dipped under his arm. The acrid smell of cigar smoke thickened the air. A short, balding man with stained teeth came out from behind a worn-looking curtain.

"Why do I have the feeling that your travel agent lied?" she whispered.

"We can always find someplace else."

Surprisingly, the room was neat and clean. The problem was that it was a single. One room. One bed. To share.

"Not exactly the way I had hoped to spend our first night together as man and wife," Lucas said, following her inside.

Marie kept her back to him as she opened her suitcase. She gave a start when he came up beside her and said his name. "Lucas…"

"No can still mean no, but does it mean I can't touch you at all?"

Marie didn't know how to answer. Parts of her

were desperate for the feel of his mouth again. It was that annoying little voice of distrust that kept her from giving an immediate response.

Lucas must have taken her silence as some sort of acquiescence. His fingers made quick work of the scarf on her head. It wasn't long before he had tossed all her hairpins on the carpet.

"You're going to have to get a second job to pay for my hairpins. I don't know why you always do that."

"Because," he breathed against her ear, "I love the way your hair feels. I love the way it smells. I love having my hands in it."

The little voice of reason in her head was getting fainter by the minute.

He left her only long enough to turn out the harsh overhead light. He drew her down onto the bed, his features shadowed in the slivers of moonlight spilling in through the window.

Lucas held his breath, afraid that this beautiful vision before him would disappear. He had only to touch her face and his desire sprang to life like a beast being awakened. Fire coiled in his gut as he drank in her subtle lilac scent.

"I should let my family know—"

He placed his finger against her rosy lips. "I called Odelle and told her where we'd be."

Marie tried to wriggle out of his grasp. "What about your job? You—"

"The hospital can page me." He draped his leg over her thighs, effectively trapping her.

"This isn't a good idea, Lucas."

He teased her earlobe with his tongue. "I think it's a wonderful idea."

"It's crazy, we hardly know each other."

"I'm going crazy," he corrected her as he tasted her skin. "Don't think, Marie. Just feel."

"This is happening too fast," she said on a ragged breath.

He trailed his lips along the elegant slope of her throat. "Any more objections?"

He heard her swallow. "No."

"Good." He sighed. "Then I'll tell you the rules."

"Rules?"

He almost laughed when he recognized that deep, sultry pitch in her voice. He waited a few minutes until he felt the tension drain from her body. It wasn't until she was pliant in his arms that he spoke again. "There aren't that many rules." He didn't really want any restrictions, not now that he felt her small fingers pressed against his chest. "The first rule is that everything we do is voluntary."

"So," Marie whispered, "if I wanted to voluntarily unbutton your shirt, that would be okay?"

"Definitely okay."

He was perfectly still while her agile fingers worked on his shirt. Tiny beads of perspiration cooled his brow, and he struggled for calm as Marie tortured him with her soft explorations. It was nothing short of a miracle that he was able to retain his control while she traced his nipple with a teasing fingertip. He almost lost it when she blew on his heated skin.

"Are there any other rules?"

"I'm beginning to regret my noble intentions," he said. "Maybe we should just forget the rules."

"No," Marie purred. "I think I like having rules. I want one of the rules to be that you can't touch me until I say so."

"I don't think I can follow that rule," he moaned.

"Yes, you can," she said, and began feathering his chest with little kisses. Her hands pushed his shirt down his arms, and she somehow managed to maneuver him so that she now straddled his waist.

Though he'd spent the preceding minutes with his eyes clamped shut, he did peer up long enough to see her. She was a vision, all wild hair and flushed cheeks. Her bracelets jingled with her every move. Lucas renewed his silent pleas for strength. If she kept this up much longer, he was afraid of the consequences.

"Not yet," she said when he reached for her.

"I'm not made of stone, Marie."

"That's debatable," she said, running her hands along his arms. "You're very hard here," she said as she touched his bicep, then her soft lips replaced her warm fingers. "And you're hard here," she continued, touching then kissing his chin. "And here." Her mouth brushed against his collarbone. "And here." The next target was his chest, just above his rapidly beating heart.

Marie wriggled lower and it was his undoing. "Game over," he rasped as his mouth closed over hers. In one lithe movement he was able to position her beneath him. She was all soft curves and sweetness. His hand slid down her leg until he captured the hem of her dress. He was afraid his kiss was too much, but when he tried to lift his head, Marie held him fast. That was all the encouragement he needed. He probably didn't even need that.

He felt like a groping teenager as he pulled at her dress. He hadn't felt this way in a lifetime. It was as though he would burn up if he couldn't have her. Nothing was going to stop him.

Nothing except the crash of breaking glass and Marie's terrified scream.

CHAPTER ELEVEN

"STAY DOWN!" LUCAS YELLED over the squeal of tires.

He raced to the door, but by the time he got it opened, the car was long gone. "Damn!"

"Are you hurt?"

"No." He turned on the light to survey the damage. "What the hell?" He reached into the shards of glass from the picture window and picked up a rock.

"What is it?" Marie asked.

"Don't walk over here, there's glass everywhere." He stepped around the glass and brought the item over to her. "I guess this is how the kids get their jollies in this backwater place."

She removed the rubber band that held a playing card to the rock. Then she blanched.

"What?" he asked, alarmed.

"It's the eight of spades."

"I can see that. Why are you so upset?"

"The eight of spades is a warning. It means evil."

Lucas snatched the card from her and tossed it into the trash. He then held her against him until she no longer trembled. "Think logically, Marie," he soothed. "A playing card can't hurt you."

"It isn't the card that has power. The card just—"

"What have you two done?" the motel manager thundered from the far side of the broken window.

Lucas straightened the opened edges of his shirt and glared at the little man. "Some idiot threw that rock through the window. It upset my wife, and that makes me *very* unhappy."

The manager's attitude changed abruptly. He offered apologies and a discount. Lucas tired of the man's ramblings and decided it was more important to get that terrified look out of Marie's eyes than waste any more time dealing with the manager.

"We'll need another room," he instructed. "Now."

A short while later, Marie stood in a new room that was a mirror reflection of the first. The card she had retrieved from the trash can was in her palm. Lucas looked from Marie to the card, his expression was of deep concern.

"Let's go find someplace for dinner," he suggested.

"I'm not very hungry."

"Maybe the smell of some good ol' chicken-fried steak will change your mind."

Marie didn't have the heart to say no. She also vowed to use the time to put her hormones back where they belonged. If it hadn't been for that rock, she knew full well what she and Lucas would be doing. That knowledge disturbed her as they walked the short distance to the restaurant.

Once they were shown to a booth, Marie continued her mental pep talk. Giving in to her body's desire for this man would be a huge mistake. She couldn't do it, knowing he didn't respect her. That undeniable fact made her sad.

"Are you a total vegetarian, or do you eat fish and chicken?" he asked, once their food had arrived.

Marie studied the mound of salad greens on the plate before her. "I eat everything but red meat."

"You aren't one of those tofu types, are you?"

She managed a smile. It was impossible not to. He was trying so hard to keep a conversation going and distract her from the unpleasant incident earlier. "I don't do tofu."

"Thank God."

"But I probably should. It *is* supposed to be good for you."

"You have my permission to bag the tofu, and I'm a doctor, so that makes it official."

"Why?"

"Why what?"

"Why did you become a doctor?"

"The usual reasons." He gave her a devilish grin. "The money."

Marie met his eyes. "Really?"

Lucas cut into his steak and grinned. "I really wanted to be a backup singer, but I can't carry a tune. The only thing I was good at was science."

"And that led to pathology?"

"Nope, I started out wanting to be a surgeon. Surgeons get all the babes."

"Be serious," she chided, though she had to admit that he had easily managed to lift her spirits.

"The truth is, I didn't choose pathology, it chose me. I did well during the rotation, liked it and decided to make it my area of concentration."

"How old are you?"

"What?" Lucas asked.

"If we're going to make the people at Haven believe us, it would probably be a good idea if I knew how old you are."

"Thirty-five."

Marie put her fork down and studied him. He had the chiseled features and warm coloring of a Nordic god. But it wasn't just his looks that made him the kind of man women noticed. Lucas had a commanding presence, even when he was relaxed. The man exuded confidence. It was probably good that he wouldn't be testifying against her.

"What about you?"

"I'm twenty-nine."

"How did you get into aromatherapy? I mean, the rest of your family seems pretty down-to-earth."

Marie felt herself frown. "I wish you wouldn't make fun of me."

Lucas leaned back, locking his fingers behind his head.

"I'm not making fun of you," he insisted. "But you must admit, aromatherapy's not exactly your average line of work."

"Do you agree that seeing is believing?"

Lucas regarded her for a moment before offering his answer. "Yes."

"The ability to see is a very powerful and effective natural sense. But smell can be just as effective."

"Smell?"

Marie tossed her hair over her shoulder. "The sense of smell has been greatly devalued in modern times. But it can be as powerful and as important as sight.''

"How?"

"People have the ability to remember scents as vividly as they remember images. Think about it. You can close your eyes and remember the smell of an ocean breeze. The scent of beer and hot dogs can trigger memories of a childhood outing to a baseball game. There are therapists who use scents to uncover repressed memories. There's a lot more to what I do than sniffing cinnamon.''

Lucas nodded. "I never said there wasn't. I think you're overly sensitive on the subject.''

She ignored his comment. "The correct balance of scents can enhance or disrupt your life. It isn't all that different from you using the correct staining agent when preparing a slide.''

"Beau wasn't kidding, was he.''

"You never know with my brother,'' Marie admitted with a genuine smile. "Can you be more specific?''

"He told me you were premed.''

"And you want to know how I went from premed to aromatherapy?''

He shrugged. "If you feel like telling me.''

"Does it matter?''

Lucas reached across the table and captured her hand in his. His eyes held hers. "Do you really find it so strange that I want to know about you? About the things that interest you?''

"Yes,'' she admitted. "You have me totally confused.''

"Why?''

"Because I can't fathom why you're going to all this trouble for me."

His thumb brushed across her knuckles. "David was my friend. I'm really a nice guy once you get to know me, and I'm partly responsible for the mess you're in."

Nothing about respect. Nothing about feelings. "That doesn't explain what almost happened back at the motel."

Lucas's gaze dropped. "I said I was a nice guy, not a saint. Look, I wish things were different."

"Getting married was your idea."

He sighed heavily. "Now I think maybe things would have been easier if we hadn't gotten married."

Hearing him say it shouldn't have hurt, but it did. She tried to pull her hand away but he resisted.

"If we weren't married, I'd know what to do."

She met his eyes. "What does that mean?"

"I'd know how to act if we were just dating. This is uncharted territory for me."

"Me, too," she admitted. "My family always says I have a knack for doing first and thinking later."

He smiled. "I hope you'll teach me to do that."

"Why?"

"Maybe opposites really do attract. I've always been the type to think a problem to death."

"Until you asked me to marry you."

His head fell to one side, and she thought she saw a flash of what was probably regret in his eyes. "You still haven't told me how you got into aromatherapy."

Smooth change of subject, she thought when he finally released her hand. "Desiree was a big influence." Marie watched as his expression soured. "What's wrong?"

"That old woman is a little hard to take."

"She's very gifted."

"As an actress," he grumbled, signaling for their check. "You don't actually buy into all that voodoo garbage, do you?"

"I've seen it work."

"Forgive me," he said. "It's just that coming from the east coast, I find the idea of believing in curses and premonitions a little hard to accept."

Marie rubbed her arms, suddenly chilled. "I know you didn't take that warning seriously, but I—"

"How well do you know Desiree?"

"What?" Marie gasped. "What are you insinuating?"

"I'm simply asking a question. Don't tell me you haven't thought of that possibility."

"What possibility?"

"Desiree provided you with the oil that killed David. Testing verified that. Did she know when you were going to search David's apartment?"

"Yes, but—"

"Did she know that we were coming to Monroe?"

"Very little goes on in my family that Desiree doesn't know about."

"Does she have any reason to want to harm you?"

Marie scoffed. "Desiree is my friend. She's taught me a great deal. She would never—"

"Who else do you know who practices voodoo?"

"This is New Orleans, Lucas. Voodoo is as much a part of our culture as Mardi Gras and jazz."

"But who else knew you would be in that motel?

Who else knew that a rock with a playing card attached to it would scare you to death?''

"Trust me, Lucas, Desiree would never do anything to harm me. She's almost like a mother to me."

"I do."

"You do what?" she asked.

"Trust you."

His compliment caught her off guard. "Thank you."

He smiled. "I like it when you blush, too."

"You're making me uncomfortable."

"Not yet, but I'd like to."

BY THE TIME THEY GOT BACK to the motel, the manager had boarded up the window and was in the process of sweeping away the fragments of glass. He grunted something as she and Lucas unlocked the door to their new room.

Marie walked into the room and stood anxiously at the end of the bed. She felt as though her entire body were strung together with taut wire. It was silly. Lucas had already proved that he could be a gentleman. Marie felt her face flush. She hadn't exactly behaved like a lady. Why did she lose all sense of propriety when the man so much as looked at her?

"Do you want the bathroom first?" she asked.

"You go ahead," he said, making a production out of checking the locks on the doors and windows.

"I'll hurry." Marie went to her suitcase and reached for the things she needed for a shower. Her hand trembled slightly.

"No need to rush. We have all the time in the world."

Did he have to speak in such a low, seductive tone? Her throat went suddenly dry—a stark contrast to the clamminess of her palms. Every muscle in her body seemed to tense with an awareness of the man just a few feet away. It was incredible. Marie didn't have casual affairs. She couldn't even recall the last time she had even been on a date. Yet Lucas had only to look at her with those sexy amber eyes and she was practically throwing herself at his feet.

Marie tossed the items she had removed back into the suitcase. Balling her hands into fists at her side, she turned and said, "This won't work. We can't stay in the same room together."

Lucas didn't respond immediately. He simply leaned against the wall as if he didn't have a care in the world. "Why not?"

Her eyes roamed boldly over the vast expanse of his shoulders and chest, and she openly admired the powerful thighs straining against the soft fabric of his jeans. The mere sight caused a fluttering in the pit of her stomach. "Because we have this…this…*this* between us." She took two breaths to calm her rapid pulse. "My self-control seems to go right out the window whenever you're around. It would be stupid for us to sleep together."

"I disagree. I want you, Marie."

"We aren't children," she insisted. "We can't have everything we want."

"Does that mean you want me, too?"

Marie closed her eyes briefly. "It means I'm very confused. It means I'm scared by the way you make me feel. It means I should be thinking about staying out of jail, but instead, I'm thinking about you."

"That's a good place to start," he said.

Marie felt herself melt at the unexpected softness in his words. She was helpless when he spoke to her like that. When he was kind and gentle, he was too perfect for words. She looked up at him. "I think it would be best if I got my own room."

"Best for whom?"

"For both of us."

"Don't speak for me, Marie. I'd like nothing more than to spend the night with you in my arms."

She glared at him. "You aren't making this any easier."

"I'm sorry," he said. He walked over and drew her into his arms. "But I'm not going to lie to you. I haven't been able to think of anything but you for days."

Protected in the circle of his arms, Marie closed her eyes and allowed her cheek to rest against his chest. Would it be so awful to take what he was so willing to give? She could forget about the trial. Forget everything but the way he made her feel. She would keep this memory in her heart always.

His fingers danced over the outline of her spine, leaving a trail of electrifying sensation in their wake. Like a spring flower, passion flourished and blossomed from deep within her, filling her quickly with a type of frenzied desire she had never before known. He ignited feelings so powerful and so intense that Marie fleetingly wondered if this was what love was like. Then he touched her and she couldn't think anymore.

Lucas moved his hand in a series of slow, sensual circles until it rested against her rib cage, just under the swell of her breast. He wanted—no, needed—to see her face. He wanted to see the desire in her eyes. Catching her chin between his thumb and forefinger, he tilted her head up with the intention of searching her eyes. He never made it that far.

His gaze was riveted to her lips, which were slightly parted, a glistening shade of pale rose. His eyes roamed over every delicate feature, and he could feel her heart rate increase. A knot formed in his throat, and he silently acknowledged his own incredible need for this woman.

Lowering his head, he was finally able to take that first tentative taste. Her mouth was warm and pliant, as was her body, which now pressed urgently against him. His hands roamed purposefully, memorizing every nuance and curve.

He felt his own body respond with an ache, then an almost overwhelming rush of desire surged through him. Her arms slid around his waist, pulling him closer. Lucas marveled at the perfect way they fit together. It was as if Marie had been made for him. For this.

"Marie," he whispered against her mouth. He toyed with a lock of her hair first, then slowly wound his hand through the silken mass and gave a gentle tug, forcing her head back even more. Looking down at her face, Lucas knew there was no other sight on earth as beautiful and inviting as her smoky blue eyes.

In one effortless motion, he lifted her and carefully lowered her onto the bed. Her dark, curly hair fanned out against the pillow.

"I think you're supposed to get on the bed with me," Marie said in a husky voice.

With a single finger, Lucas traced the delicate outline of her mouth. Her skin was the color of ivory, with a faint rosy flush. "Are you sure?" he asked in a tight voice, not certain how he would handle it if she uttered a rejection. He sucked in a breath and waited for her response.

"Very."

Sliding onto the bed with her, he began showering her face and neck with light kisses. While his mouth searched for that sensitive spot at the base of her throat, he felt her fingers working the buttons of his shirt.

He waited breathlessly for the feel of her hands on his body, and he wasn't disappointed when the anticipation gave way to reality. A pleasurable moan spilled from his mouth as she brushed away his clothing and began running her palms over the taut muscles of his stomach.

Capturing both of her hands in one of his, Lucas gently held them above her head. The position arched her back, drawing his eyes down to the outline of her erect nipples.

"This isn't fair," she said as he slowly undid the buttons of her dress.

"Believe me, Marie. If I let you keep touching me, I'd probably last less than a minute."

Marie responded by lifting her body to him. The rounded swell of one breast brushed his arm. He began peeling away her layers of clothing and was rewarded by the incredible sight of her breasts spilling over the edges of a lacy undergarment. His eyes burned as he drank in the sight of the taut peaks straining against the lace. His hand rested first against the flatness of her stomach before inching up over her warm flesh. Finally, his fingers closed over the rounded fullness of her breast.

"Please let me touch you!" Marie cried out.

"Not yet," he whispered, releasing the front clasp on her bra. He ignored her futile struggle to free her hands and dipped his head to kiss the raging pulse point at her throat. Her soft skin grew hot as he worked his mouth lower and lower. She gasped when his mouth closed around her nipple, then she called his name in a hoarse voice that caused a tremor to run the full length of his body.

Moments later, he lifted his head only long enough to see her passion-ladened expression and to tell her she was beautiful.

"So are you."

Whether it was the sound of her voice or the way she pressed herself against him, Lucas didn't know or care. He found himself nearly undone by the intense passion she communicated with the movements of her supple body.

He reached down until his fingers made contact with a wisp of silk and lace. The feel of the sensuous garment against his skin nearly pushed him over the edge. With her help, he was able to whisk the panties over her hips and legs, until she was finally next to him without a single barrier.

He sought her mouth again and released his hold on her hands. He didn't know which was more potent, the feel of her naked body against his or the frantic way she worked to remove his clothing. His body moved to cover hers, his tongue thrust deeply into the warm recesses of her mouth. His hand skimmed over her hip, all the way to her thigh. Then, giving in to the urgent need pulsating through him, Lucas positioned himself between her legs. Every muscle in his body tensed as he looked down at her face. Marie flattened her palms against his hips and tugged him toward her, welcoming, inviting.

"I wish it could be this way forever," he groaned against her lips.

"Don't think about forever," she whispered back. "Not now. Just make love to me, please?"

He wasted no time responding to her request. In a single motion, he thrust deeply inside her, knowing without question that he had found heaven on earth.

He wanted to treat her to a slow, building climax, but with the strength of the feelings sweeping through him, that wasn't an option. He caught his breath and held it. The sheer pleasure of being inside her sweet softness was too powerful. She wrapped her legs around his hips just as the first explosive waves surged through him. One after the other, ripples of pleasure poured from him into her. Satisfaction had never been so sweet.

With his head buried next to hers, he breathed in the fragrant scent of her hair. It took several minutes before his heartbeat slowed to a steady pace. Never in his life had he felt so content.

Rolling onto his side, Lucas rested his head against his arm and glanced down at her. Alarm filled him when he saw the stricken look in her eyes.

"What's wrong?" he asked. Then, seeing the flush of unspent passion, he reached for her.

She slapped his hand away.

"I'm only human, Marie," he said as guilt filled him. "Lie still and I'll make you feel better."

The color in her cheeks intensified to match the smoldering anger in her eyes. "I don't want you to touch me. Ever again."

"Marie!" he called as she sprang from the bed and barricaded herself in the bathroom. He let out a string of expletives. Locking herself into the bathroom was becoming an art form with Marie.

When he no longer heard the shower, Lucas pulled on his jeans and waited at the end of the bed.

Marie emerged wearing a bathrobe, the edges pulled up to her throat. She wouldn't look at him. After tossing the towel aside, she moved to the head of the bed. "Here," she snapped, and threw a pillow at his head.

Lucas caught the pillow as he was getting up. "What am I supposed to do with this?"

"Sleep."

"Marie," he began patiently, "I know I was a little selfish, but if you'll give me a chance, I'll make it up to you."

Her eyes were narrowed, like silver thunderclouds about to explode. "Selfish? Try careless."

Lucas tossed the pillow into a nearby chair and raked his fingers through his hair. "Careless?"

"Neither of us gave a thought to protection," Marie muttered as she stripped the bed of its blanket. Wadding it into a ball, she threw the blanket in his general direction.

Lucas studied her face. "Marie, what's this all about?" Marie didn't meet his gaze but simply stood next to the bed. Lucas went over to her and gathered her against him. He gently stroked her back until he felt some of the tension drain from her small body. "Now, want to tell me what is really bothering you?"

"I don't know," she cried. "I'm totally confused. Worse than before."

Lucas kissed the top of her head. "Everything will work out."

"Why are you so nice to me even when I'm being an emotional shrew?"

"I told you already, I'm a nice guy."

"This would be easier if you weren't."

Lucas glanced heavenward. "I know." He lay down on the bed and held her until her breathing slowed and became rhythmic. He followed her into sleep a long time later, still not sure whether making love to her had been the right move. Maybe Marie was right. Maybe it was all happening too fast.

"I WANT YOU OUT OF HERE."

"Excuse me?" Marie said to the motel manager. She was returning from a trip to the restaurant for coffee the following morning when he intercepted her, a nasty expression on his face.

"We don't like your kind here."

"My kind?"

He snapped a newspaper from under his pudgy arm and practically threw it at her. "I don't need no killers here."

Marie blinked disbelievingly and felt her jaw drop. A banner headline read Marie's Motive Revealed. Beneath the type was a huge photograph of her and David Markum. It was the same picture Lucas had shown her on Christmas Eve.

"That bastard," she whispered.

CHAPTER TWELVE

"THANKS A LOT," she snapped, tossing the paper into his lap.

Still groggy, Lucas rubbed his eyes before he was able to focus on the newspaper.

"I can't believe this," he said a minute later.

"Why not? It's all your fault that Carl Lee got his hands on that picture to begin with."

"I couldn't exactly destroy it, Marie. The wallet and everything in it are evidence." Lucas read the article. "It says here that the district attorney is considering an amendment to your charge."

"I have you to thank for that."

Lucas let out a breath. She was right. If he hadn't let Carl Lee dictate to him, he could have done a more thorough investigation. And yet, at that moment, he wished that he had never even bothered to run the tox screen. Then David's death might never have been classified as a murder. He moved to Marie, not completely sure how to approach her. She was looking at him with such contempt. It didn't seem possible that just hours ago she had been in his arms. "I didn't know Carl Lee would use the photograph like this."

Marie reached up and touched his cheek. "I'm sorry, Lucas. I know this isn't you fault. I just wanted a hate object and you were handy. Temper is a Delacroix trait and curse.''

"I'll remember that in the future.''

"Judging by this story, I don't have a future.''

Lucas gave her a quick kiss. "Why don't you call Shelby and find out how much of that is sensationalism and how much is fact.''

"Good idea,'' she said, forcing a smile.

He would have given anything to be able to erase that haunted look from her eyes. It amazed him how strongly he felt. It also scared him. Maybe a shower would clear his mind. Maybe hell would freeze over.

MARIE WAS DISTRACTED by the sounds of the shower. Or more accurately, she was distracted by the man in the shower. She should have been concentrating on this new development in her case, but her mind had a different agenda.

Last night had been a turning point. Why had she made love to him? The answer that sprang to mind positively terrified her. She couldn't fall in love with a man who didn't respect her. She shouldn't. Maybe she already had.

"What did Shelby say?''

She worked to keep the catch of emotion from her voice. There was no point in complicating the situation any further. No point in making herself more vulnerable. "She's filing some sort of motion to request a gag order. But the papers are free to print whatever they want—unless it's actually libelous. The daughter of a judge being charged with murder sells papers. Shelby doesn't think we've seen the last of it.''

"Will the gag order help?"

"Probably not," she answered curtly. "She also said it wasn't such a swift idea for us to be going to Haven."

"Did she have a better suggestion?"

"Not really. But if all else fails, I can take the plea the D.A. has offered. Five to fifteen years."

"Don't be ridiculous."

"I could get twice that from a jury."

"Damn it, Marie! You aren't going to jail."

"Don't be so sure. But look on the bright side, you'll get a divorce decree faster if I'm in jail." She had meant it to sound light, casual, but by the time she finished the sentence she was crying.

"Please don't cry," Lucas said as he held her. "I've never been any good with women's tears. They make me feel so inadequate."

Marie sniffed, keeping her cheek against his tear-dampened chest. "I don't think anything could make you feel inadequate."

"You do," he said softly. "I feel so responsible for all this, and I don't know how to make it right."

Marie didn't want his guilt. Or his pity. Gently, she stepped from his embrace. "It isn't your fault," she said without looking at him. "You'd better finish getting dressed. We don't want to be late getting to Haven."

It took Lucas no time to dress, pack the car and have a final word with the motel manager. True to his word, the drive to their destination was less than thirty minutes.

Haven Cottages was located on a rolling piece of land near a small stream. The grounds were naturally landscaped, the cabins rustic and symmetrically aligned around a larger central building. It seemed peaceful, idyllic...and not a very likely place to find a killer.

Lucas pulled his car up to the gatehouse and was greeted by an energetic young woman who said, "Park over there, please. Harry will take your things to your cabin. We're glad to have you with us. And congratulations, Graham said you were newlyweds."

"Thanks," Lucas replied smoothly as he placed his hand on Marie's leg.

Why did that simple action cause her heart to flutter? Why did it feel so right? She wasn't going to let anything happen again until she had figured out why this man had such an effect on her. For once in her life, she was going to ignore her instincts and use her brain. She only wished her body was as determined as her mind.

Marie and Lucas were shown to a large barn-shaped building marked Main Hall. Inside, it resembled a huge log cabin, though a close inspection revealed that the primitive-looking logs were nothing more than a facade. Like her marriage.

Stop it! she chided herself. *Concentrate. You're here to find the real killer.*

Long tables filled half the space, and the other half looked like a relaxation area. Overstuffed chairs were arranged in a semicircle, large throw pillows nearly covered the carpeting. The room smelled like bacon and sawdust. Marie suddenly wanted to leave. "I don't know if I can act well enough to pull this off."

"We've come this far," Lucas whispered against her ear. "We can't leave now."

"I just don't know if I can go through with this," she said. "Maybe I should forget all about it and leave everything to Shelby."

"Beau said you were a fighter. Are you?"

"When I have a shot at winning," she told him. "I'm bright enough to know when I'm in over my head."

His hand went to her waist and he pulled her to his side. "Don't sell yourself short. This whole nightmare will go away if we can find the killer."

Marie gripped his hand in hers. "I hope so," she murmured. The nightmare wouldn't be the only thing that went away, she thought with a sinking heart. So would Lucas.

The schedule at Haven Cottages made Marie feel as if she was back in summer camp. There was an organized breakfast, then something called a Trust Encounter. Lunch was optional, but like all meals was served in the Main Hall. The afternoon had such intriguing options as Communication Essentials and Massage Techniques. "Do we all wear matching outfits?" Marie joked as soon as she and Lucas were alone in their cabin.

"I hope not," he said.

There was something in his tone that caught her attention. She looked up to find him staring out the window. He seemed tense, coiled.

"What's wrong?"

Marie was doubly worried when he turned around and she saw the deep lines of strain marring his features. "Look," she began, only to be silenced by his uplifted hand.

"I've been thinking. It would probably be best if we didn't...repeat last night."

Marie was stunned by his sudden and unexpected proclamation. Her astonishment must have shown on her face because he immediately offered a smile. "That's fine," she said in an amazingly placid tone.

Lucas chuckled. "I'm not saying I don't want to. It's just that you've got so much on your plate now, I don't think it's a wise idea to complicate the situation."

Marie should have been relieved. She wasn't. "Okay."

Her eyes followed him as he left the cabin. When the door closed, she felt a chill all the way to her core.

She unpacked her suitcase, and as she worked, she kept looking down at her wedding ring. After closing one of the drawers, she held her left hand up to the light. The ring was beautiful. The diamonds sparkled and cast prisms of color all over the walls. How much longer would she be able to wear it, she wondered sadly.

Forty minutes passed, then an hour, and still no Lucas. Marie had explored all three rooms of the cabin. The decor was reminiscent of the television series "Little House on the Prairie," and the kitchenette was designed for little more than mixing drinks and boiling water. The small living area was cozy, in a woodsy way. The sofa was small, and there were throw pillows tossed around it. Against one wall was a fireplace. Going to her dresser, she carefully removed a plastic case and placed it on the bed. After she opened it, she got out the Seven Candles of the

Spectrum and a small vial and took them into the living room.

Kicking off her shoes, she arranged the different colored candles in a circle on the hearth and sat in front of them, the small glass vial in her hand. Once she had lit the candles, she removed the stopper from the bottle and took small whiffs of the camphor. The scented oil took a while to work, but she continued to breathe slowly, and at last her tense body relaxed.

"WE'RE SUPPOSED TO ATTEND the lectures," Lucas whispered when she started to walk back in the direction of their cabin after a late lunch.

"You go. I'm tired of listening to Graham Nash and his perpetually positive take on married life. I feel like I'm trapped in some sort of long-playing info-mercial for wedded bliss."

"Stop whining," Lucas said with a chuckle. "Communication or massage?"

"Communication," she answered quickly. Maybe too quickly, if that smug smile of his was any indication.

For the third time that day, Marie found herself seated in a semicircle with a handful of other couples. Some, like the Duvalls, sat close together like a couple of teenagers. Mrs. Duvall seemed most content when she was seated in Mr. Duvall's lap. Other couples held hands or sat at their partner's feet. Only Marie and Lucas opted to sit side by side.

"Welcome to Communication Essentials," Graham Nash said as he entered the room. He was enthusiastic and loud, like a fifty-something cheerleader. Marie had recognized him the minute she saw him again. Luckily, he had given no indication that he remembered her. But maybe that was because he had something to hide....

"Mrs. Henderson?"

"I—I'm sorry," she stammered. "What did you ask?"

"I asked you to tell me one positive way and one negative way your husband communicates his feelings."

"In the negative," Marie began, in spite of the pressure Lucas was applying to her hand, "Lucas jumps to conclusions before he has all the facts. He says the first thing that comes to his mind, no matter how painful or destructive that thought could turn out to be. He claims to be an honest man, but—"

"Thank you, Mrs. Henderson," Graham interrupted gently. "Now share something positive."

Marie frowned, pursing her lips as she thought. "He has a decent vocabulary."

She managed to steal a glimpse at Lucas. Fuming mad was a pretty apt description.

"Can you expand on that?" Graham pressed.

"In all the time we've been together, I've never heard him mispronounce a word."

There were a few snickers from the other couples. The pressure of Lucas's grip was beginning to hurt. It wasn't nearly as bad as the pained expression Graham now donned.

"Did I say something wrong?" she asked with feigned innocence.

"There is no wrong here," Graham reminded her. "But I'm sensing some hostility from you. Would you like to share some of it?"

"Not particularly," she said, matching his saccharine smile with one of her own.

"Perhaps *you* would like to comment, Dr. Henderson?"

Marie braced herself. Lucas would probably give it to her with both barrels. "My wife is having a difficult adjustment to married life."

"Is that true?" Graham asked Marie.

She felt herself tense. "It *is* very...different from what I expected."

Graham nodded seriously, as if she had just divulged some huge secret. "That is quite common."

"The first year is the best and the worst," Mrs. Duvall chimed in. "My advice is to spend most of it in bed."

That remark caused the group to cackle like hens.

"Thank you, Louise," Lucas said. "That sounds like good advice."

"This is good," Graham said. "Let's move on to the concept of physical communication between husband and wife."

"That won't be a very long discussion for us," Marie whispered cattily.

"What was that?" Graham asked.

"Nothing," Marie answered, coloring.

Graham regarded her for a long time, then turned to the other couples. By the end of the session, Marie knew more about this group of strangers than she ever really wanted to know. When Louise started to relate a sexual encounter in an RV, Marie was thrilled when Graham interrupted. She wasn't sure if she was envious or embarrassed. She just knew she was very uncomfortable listening to virtual strangers discuss the most intimate details of their lives.

"I want you all to go back to your cabins."

"Thank God," Marie whispered.

Lucas pinched her.

"I want you to find an effective method of non-verbal communication."

"Any kind?" Louise asked hopefully.

"No talking," Graham said. "And no rules."

Rules. The word caused Marie to flush. A vivid memory of Lucas teasing her with rules and caresses flashed in her mind.

"Are you all right, Mrs. Henderson?"

"Yes."

"Are you sure, Marie?" Lucas taunted. Then, lowering his voice, he asked, "Do you want to share?"

Marie ground her teeth together. The whole group was looking at her now. "I must be tired from the trip."

Graham nodded. "Go with that. Build from there. Sharing a late afternoon nap in a secluded place is a wonderful nonverbal exercise."

"You didn't exactly blend in back there," Lucas chided as they walked toward their cabin.

She remembered all too well Lucas's edict about the previous night. Well, if he wasn't interested in making love, neither was she. Much. "The only nonverbal thing I want to do with you is take a peek into the office files."

Lucas quickened his pace, pulling her along with him.

"What's your hurry?" she demanded.

"I'm afraid someone will overhear you and find

out why we're really here," he said as they entered the cabin.

"So, how long do we play touchy-feely with Dr. Nash and his buddies? Don't you find these sessions annoying?"

Lucas went to the small refrigerator and got a beer. His eyes met hers and he shrugged. "I'm learning."

"Learning what? These people are perfect candidates for divorce. Mr. Duvall cares more about his bowling league than he does about his wife."

"His wife only cares about one thing," Lucas remarked with a lecherous smile.

Marie grinned, too, in spite of herself. "I didn't know women in their seventies were so...so..."

"Interested?"

"Needy," Marie corrected him. "She acts as if they haven't been together in years. She's a grandmother, for goodness' sake."

Lucas tossed his head back and laughed. "Grandmothers enjoy sex, too."

"Not my grandmothers."

Quietly, he finished the beer, and all the time his eyes seemed to follow her. All that attention was making her nervous.

"You're a hard woman to figure out, Marie."

"Me?" she scoffed, twisting a lock of hair around her finger.

"Yep." He stretched his long body and rolled his head around on his shoulders. "I'm going to take Nash's advice."

"What?" she asked, reflexively grabbing the neckline of her dress.

Lucas regarded her action with something that

looked very much like disappointment but was more likely fatigue. "I'm going to take a nap."

"But we need to look around!"

"We will," he promised. "After I take a nap." Turning his back to her, he walked over to the bed and lay down.

So much for communication, Marie thought with a huff. Verbal or otherwise.

CHAPTER THIRTEEN

IT WAS DARK when Lucas awoke. He stretched out on the bed, his heart stopping when his knee bumped into something soft and warm.

"Marie?" he mumbled.

"Hmm?"

Almost reflexively, Lucas reached out and curved his arm around her, then pulled her against him. Her legs straightened, bringing their bodies together beneath the soft down comforter. When her wild hair brushed against his cheek, all the hours of wanting and waiting fueled a fire within him that threatened his resolve not to complicate his relationship with Marie. Turning his face into her hair, Lucas drank in the scent of honeysuckle and reached up to lace his fingers in the silky mass.

It felt so right that he braved a gentle, tentative kiss against the warm skin of her forehead. Everything stopped—time, his heartbeat, his breathing—as he braced for rejection.

Marie drew back far enough to meet his eyes. "Lucas?" she whispered.

"Yes."

"The camphor didn't work."

"Is this some sort of riddle?" he moaned. "I'm

having a hard time thinking rationally. I'm not even sure finding you in my bed isn't a dream.''

"No dream," she assured him with a kiss. "I called Desiree. She did a reading for me and made some suggestions.''

"What kind of suggestions?''

"The camphor, for one.''

"That stuff you were sniffing earlier?''

"Yes. Desiree reminded me that it promotes celibacy.''

"Do you really think I want to discuss celibacy when you're in my arms?''

Her mouth opened slowly and his tongue slipped between her teeth. His initial trepidation was forgotten as she kissed him deeply, completely. The inside of her mouth was delicious and warm. He explored her with his tongue before drawing her bottom lip between his teeth and teasing her gently. She responded by making a small guttural sound, and her hands began to knead his chest through his shirt. As his tongue glided across her lips, he felt her hands tugging at his T-shirt, then her fingers combed through his chest hair and her nails gently raked his nipples.

Her movements were tentative, almost shy, which seemed at odds with the searing passion of her kisses. Lucas shifted, rolling her on top of him so that he could feel every inch of her soft flesh. His hand went to her breast, teasing and taunting the heated flesh through her lacy bra. His lips found her neck in the darkness and he kissed and nibbled, tilting her at will with the hand he had entwined in her hair.

Her breast filled his hand, and she responded with

a small shiver when he ran his thumb across the taut nipple. Shifting again so that he lay half on top of her, Lucas quickly shed boxers and T-shirt, then eased past the barrier of panties and bra. The feel of naked flesh against naked flesh made his body burn like a furnace and he willed himself to slow the pace. This time he was determined to make it something she would enjoy. His hand slid down over the side of her full breast, over the gentle curve of her waist to the hard outline of her hipbone. When he explored farther, to the satiny smoothness of her thigh, Marie arched her back, sighing.

The realization that her need was as great as his own was almost more sensual that the tiny circles she was tracing on his skin. Lucas gathered her beneath him. He paused, his eyes riveted to her face and the flush of passion he saw there. His chest swelled with purely masculine pride. Marie's desire for him made him feel like a man. But he was a man running low on control.

"I'm sorry," he whispered as he positioned himself above her.

"Sorry for what?" She reached up and brushed the hair from his forehead.

"I'm sorry I didn't make it right for you last night."

Marie's sigh sounded much like the purr of a contented cat. "I think I'm sorry, too."

Lucas buried himself in the sheath of her body. Watching her expressions change and evolve, he adjusted his rhythm accordingly. He wanted so much to sustain the pleasure, to make it last forever. It took Herculean strength of will to wait for her signal. Her head arched against the pillow, her eyes squeezed shut. He felt her body grow stiff, then a powerful climax claimed them both.

"WE MISSED YOU at dinner," Louise Duvall chirped when Lucas and Marie entered the Main Hall arm in arm.

Marie felt her face flame. She would have bolted from the room but for Lucas's death grip on her waist.

"Were you two communicating nonverbally?" Louise asked with a wink.

"I'm outta here," Marie groaned, trying to break free.

"I'm so sorry, dear," Louise said quickly. "Does my teasing upset you? I'm just funning."

"It's no problem," Lucas assured the woman. "Marie is just a little uncomfortable with so much openness."

"You should be married to my Dale," Louise said. "He gets embarrassed when I hang his drawers on the line."

"Can we see if there's anything left for dinner?" Marie pleaded. "I'm famished."

"Worked up an appetite, did you?" Louise called after them.

"It's a good thing for that woman that I am *not* a murderer. One more comment and I'd gladly strangle her with the clothesline she hangs her poor husband's underwear on."

Lucas's chuckle was deep and masculine. A lot like the way he made love.

A very attentive waiter was kind enough to go into the kitchen and fix them plates from the now dismantled buffet. They sat across from each other, segregated from the small boisterous groups.

"You're staring," Marie accused him.

"I'm confused," Lucas said.

"Basil essential oil used sparingly should help."

He responded with a sidelong glance.

"Don't knock it until you've tried it."

His smile had the power to steal her breath. "I might just surprise you and take you up on that." He glanced around, then leaned forward. Her hands were swallowed by his. "Last night you said—"

"I said a lot of things last night," Marie admitted. *I also didn't say the one thing I should have.* "You should learn to ignore me at times, Lucas. Talking to Desiree helped me regain my perspective."

"Perspective on what? And why does it bother me that you only came to me after a long-distance pep talk from a sideshow psychic?"

Marie tugged her hands free. "It isn't fair for you to condemn Desiree. It also isn't very smart." *Especially since she told me why I react to you the way I do.*

"I apologize. If I'm willing to entertain the idea that Desiree's talents are genuine, can I have a kiss?"

"No. But are you willing?"

Lucas winked. "And able."

"Get your brain out of the gutter. I should have asked her about the card I got."

"Why didn't you?"

"I didn't want to upset her."

Lucas held her gaze. "Seriously, Marie—is there any possibility that she could be involved?"

Marie bristled. "No."

Lucas brushed his thumb across her palm. "Then, we won't mention it again. I trust your judgment. Who else could have had access to the oils in your shop? Or knew your schedule? Whoever killed David had to know both of you well." Lucas raked his fingers through his freshly washed hair. "Okay, maybe it has something to do with the fact that you dated David. Maybe he had a jealous former lover." Lucas's eyes narrowed. "Or maybe you did?"

"Sorry. No. But David mentioned a woman to me a couple of weeks ago."

Lucas looked hopeful. "Who was she?"

"He never said her name. I'm not sure he was even seeing her. It was almost as if he was describing his ideal woman."

"Did she have dark hair and eyes the color of a storm?"

To her credit, Marie managed to choke down part of a baked potato. How could a single question raise her blood pressure through the roof? How would she be able to walk away when this was over? At least she hadn't followed all of Desiree's advice. She hadn't told him she was falling in love with him. She needed to think.

"ARE WE BACK to the silent treatment?" Lucas asked as they prepared to go to the evening discussion on trust.

"I don't have anything to say."

Lucas grabbed her arm, making it impossible for her to finish making the bed. "They have people who will do that for us."

She didn't look at him. It was too dangerous. "I

don't like being idle. I'm used to working all day, not sitting cross-legged, tittering about other people's problems.''

"Can you titter, Marie?" he teased. "I've never heard you titter.''

She refused to be drawn in by his seductive tone and the gentle stroke of his thumb just inside her elbow. She couldn't think straight when he touched her. When he wielded that smile like a weapon. When he dispensed his considerable charm.

Lucas nibbled her earlobe. "We have some time before the session. We could— Ouch!''

Marie took refuge on the opposite side of the bed. Lucas looked positively murderous as he rubbed his instep. "I'm sorry. I didn't mean to hit you that hard. But I can't think when you touch me. Even you said we shouldn't complicate things.''

"Do you know how hard it is to have your own words used against you?" he complained through clenched teeth.

"But you might have been right," Marie said. "We missed dinner. We missed an opportunity to learn something from the other guests.''

His shoulders slumped forward. "You're right. It won't happen again.''

"Fine.''

"Fine.''

There was something final in his tone. When she heard it, her heart sank.

She didn't feel fine after he slammed out of the bedroom. It took her three attempts to tie her scarf because she was so distracted. Well, Desiree might have seen Lucas as Marie's destiny. Marie thought he might just be her downfall.

Going to the closet, she pulled a new dress off its hanger. It was simple, bias cut, made of a silk blend that flowed from her shoulders to her feet, drenching her in swirls of red and hot pink, accented with some green and gold beads. From the suitcase, she found her jewelry and began the long process of adding earrings, bracelets and necklaces to her outfit. Just before she gathered the strength to join Lucas, she touched up her makeup.

The extra care wasn't lost on him. Not if his expression was any indication. Marie told herself she shouldn't be pleased.

"How do you do that?" he asked as he shrugged into a jacket.

"Do what?"

"You put together colors and accessories that should look awful, but you pull it off."

Marie held his gaze as she reached for the doorknob. Her only defense against her own need was the pretext that she didn't care. "Are you ready?"

Her aloofness seemed to do the trick. Lucas didn't bother with another compliment. In fact, for the first time since their arrival, he didn't touch her when they joined the others for the evening session.

Marie took her usual seat to the far right. The Duvalls and the Stapletons were chatting with Graham Nash. As expected, Lucas went and got one of the folding chairs and brought it over in her general direction. Unlike the previous times, he left enough space between them to park a small car. The tension they generated was almost palpable, and Marie was giving serious consideration to leaving. She could go back to the cabin, wait until the middle of the night, find the office, have a look around and be gone before dawn. She told herself that she didn't need Lucas. But she knew she did.

Graham broke off his conversation with the older couples, and Marie knew she would have to make her exit quickly. As inconspicuously as possible, she rose from her chair and turned toward the door.

"You aren't leaving?" Graham said at the same instant that Lucas grabbed her wrist and pulled her into his lap.

Thanks to the two men, Marie was now the central focus of the small group. Lucas still held her wrist in his viselike grip, and his shimmering amber eyes fairly dared her to challenge him.

"Just getting comfortable," she lied.

"Now I know who you are!" Ginger Stapleton announced with pure venom in her eyes. "You had your hair down before!"

"I'm sorry?" Marie said politely.

"I kept telling Wayne that I knew you from somewhere. Now that you're all done up, I recognize you. You're that rich girl from New Orleans that killed David."

There were several strangled cries, then Marie felt a dozen pairs of angry eyes turn on her. It reminded her of the courthouse and her arraignment. The only difference was the protective way Lucas held her in the crook of his arm.

"C'mon," he whispered. "I think we just blew our cover."

CHAPTER FOURTEEN

GRAHAM NASH SAT behind an impressive wooden desk, his fingers steepled, his expression stern. "I must admit that I am surprised that you would come here, Mrs. Henderson. Though it does explain why you never volunteered your real name."

"That is her real name," Lucas said, meeting the other man's pensive stare. "Marie and I were married on Christmas Eve. I provided all the necessary documentation to your staff."

"I read the New Orleans papers, Doctor."

"Lucas?" Marie began. He silenced her with a single look.

"That doesn't mean you know the truth."

Graham gave a slight nod. "I know the district attorney believes that this woman killed David. I also know that she and David had a relationship."

Lucas rose and paced the carpeted floor. "Do you know who I am?"

"Only what you've shared with the group. You're a pathologist at a hospital in New Orleans."

Lucas allowed his gaze rest on Marie. She sat primly in the chair, her hands folded neatly in her lap. The knowledge that she wouldn't be in this situation if it wasn't for him was gnawing at his insides like a cancer.

"David Markum was my roommate in college."

A light of recognition dawned in the man's eyes. "I recall David mentioning you."

"Then you should understand that I wouldn't be with Marie if I thought she was responsible for my friend's death."

"That would be unusual, but not unheard of. Forgive me, Mrs. Henderson," he said, then turned his attention back to Lucas. "Your wife is a beautiful woman. It also isn't unusual for men to be blinded by beauty."

"I'm not swayed by her looks," Lucas insisted. "I don't need a trophy wife."

Graham conceded the point with a slight flicker of his eyes. The clock on the wall chimed, giving Lucas a chance to improvise an argument. "After Marie was charged, I found some inconsistencies in the evidence."

"Then shouldn't you have taken your reservations to the proper authorities? Why come here?"

"We wanted to—" Marie began.

"Understand what David did for a living," Lucas finished for her. "We were hoping it might explain some of the inconsistencies."

"Such as?" Graham queried.

Lucas was being squeezed between a rock and a hard place. There was a possibility that Nash was somehow involved. Maybe even the killer. There was nothing to be gained by tipping their hand.

"We wanted to know how personal the sessions are," Marie answered smoothly. "Since neither of us has ever been married, we didn't know how a place like Haven worked."

"You could have written to me. I would have supplied you with a brief outline of our services."

Marie reached out to Lucas and took his hand, squeezing it lightly before she continued speaking. "I'm in the indelicate position of being pressed for time. With the trial just around the corner, we thought it would be easier to just make the trip. We also hoped it might help us get through the trying times we're facing."

Graham's expression grew softer and more compassionate as Marie lulled him with her voice. "I suppose it was unfortunate that Mrs. Stapleton recognized you. This is the third year they have joined us for marriage enhancement. They used to work closely with David on the rare occasions he came up here."

"Wha—"

"We'll leave in the morning," Lucas said, keeping his expression neutral. "We're very sorry if we disrupted your session. That was never our intention." He almost had to yank Marie out of her chair. It was only by sending her a silent warning that he was able to keep her quiet.

Graham stood and extended his hand. "David thought a great deal of you, Marie. He was always singing your praises to our clients. If you didn't kill him, then I wish you the best of luck. If you did, God help you."

"He already has," Lucas returned with a casual smile. "We really are sorry if we disrupted anything."

"YOU'RE SORRY." Marie seethed when they were back inside their cabin. "You are sorry!"

Lucas chuckled at her, which didn't improve her disposition.

"I fail to see the humor in this. Nash said David came up here infrequently. If that was true, he was definitely doing something funny on his taxes."

"Maybe," Lucas said, stroking his chin. "We won't know for a few hours yet."

She tilted her chin back to meet his eyes. "What difference will a few hours make?"

"As soon as we're sure everyone is down for the count, we can go have a look at the offices."

"Don't you think Nash might be expecting us to do that?"

"It's a chance we're going to have to take."

Marie touched the back of his hand. "*Why* are we going to take a risk like that?"

"Because I saw something on Nash's desk that has me curious."

"What?"

"A phone number."

"And that has you all worked up? Did you recognize the number?"

"I'm not sure."

"Then why is it important? Would you care to share?" she asked, imitating the counselor's oft-used phrase.

Lucas laughed. "Not until I'm certain. I can't be sure until I can see the number right side up and try it with a New Orleans area code."

His fingers reached up and grasped her shoulders. His grip bit into her flesh. He opened his mouth as if to speak, then abruptly he released her and marched into the bedroom, slamming the door with enough force to rattle the paintings on the walls.

Marie sat alone in the living room, her bare feet tucked under her. How had things gotten so complicated, she wondered for the umpteenth time. She let her breath out slowly and twisted her wedding band around her finger. Her heart felt heavy and sadness filled her.

What if they had met under different circumstances?

What if he hadn't been there for her during Charly's ordeal?

What if they hadn't rushed into this sham wedding?

What if he respected her?

What if she wasn't falling in love with him?

Afraid she might slip into an even deeper funk, she picked up the telephone and called Beau.

"Hello?"

"Did I wake you?" she asked quickly.

"What time is it?"

"A little after one."

"Then you woke me," Beau grumbled good-naturedly. "Is everything okay?"

"Sure," she replied. "I just wanted to know how Daddy took the article in this morning's paper."

"Better than he took the news of your marriage. He's threatening to sue," Beau supplied, sounding more alert now. "How's married life?"

"Exactly as I thought it would be."

There was a brief silence before he said, "C'mon, Marie. This is me, I know when you're upset. If Lucas has—"

"Lucas isn't the problem," Marie assured him. "I

just got a little homesick and I wanted to make sure Charly was still improving.''

"She's chomping at the bit to get released from the hospital.''

"Give her a kiss for me.''

"I think she'd rather have an explanation.''

"For what?''

Marie heard the rustling of sheets. "She doesn't understand your quick plunge into matrimony. Neither does the rest of the family.''

"How's Daddy doing?''

"You know how he gets when one of his own is in trouble. By the way, Shelby called here and said that the judge granted her motion for a gag order. There won't be any more quotes from the D.A. in the paper.''

"That's something,'' Marie murmured. "She didn't happen to say if she'd had any luck with the license plate of that woman I told you about.''

"The plates were for a rental,'' Beau answered. "She said she would try to see if she can get a name from the agency.''

"Thanks. I'd better go.''

"Wait, Marie?''

"Yes?''

"Are you sure you're okay?''

She rubbed her eyes. "I'm fine. Is there any good family gossip I'm missing out on?''

"Aunt Mary is getting stronger every day,'' he said. "She's worried about Uncle Philip. He's convinced he's been cursed and that he's going to die and that Grandfather is behind it. Not that any of this is really news.''

Marie laughed. "I should probably go."

"What's wrong?"

Marie hesitated, then forced a lightness into her voice. "Nothing, why?"

"Because newlyweds don't call their big brothers in the middle of the night unless something is wrong."

"I've got to go."

She heard him give a heavy sigh. "If Lucas has done something to you, I'd be happy to kick his butt."

"No need," Marie assured him, touched by his concern. "Everything will work out."

"Does that mean you've discovered something up there?"

"Yes and no," she hedged. "We're coming back to New Orleans in the morning."

"You're being evasive, Marie. What did you find out?"

"Later, Beau," she said, and placed the receiver on the cradle.

"Who were you talking to?"

Hello to you, too, she thought, mild irritation and disappointment replacing her melancholy. "Beau was filling me in on the case and some family stuff."

Lucas looked furious. "You haven't told him that we—"

"No, Lucas. I don't discuss my personal life with my brother."

"Good, because I don't relish the idea of your brother coming after me when this is all over. This whole mess is already complicated enough."

A complicated mess. Well, Marie thought wryly. She had to give Lucas credit. He certainly had a way with words....

CHAPTER FIFTEEN

"SORRY," THEY WHISPERED in unison when Lucas's arm brushed against her back in the darkness.

Marie swallowed. She was a bundle of raw nerves. "I don't know if I can do it in the dark."

"We don't have a choice."

His breath warmed her earlobe. It was hard to concentrate with him almost on top of her. She could hardly keep her hand steady—a definite must if she was going to pick the lock.

"Can you speed it up?" Lucas asked.

"I'm doing my best!" she snapped. A few seconds later, they were safely inside the office where, hours earlier, Nash had delivered his lecture.

Lucas moved to the desk, a penlight in his teeth, and Marie followed the narrow beam with her eyes.

"Damn," he muttered softly.

"What?"

"The phone number isn't here anymore. Nash must have destroyed it."

Marie walked toward him, careful to keep a safe distance. If she couldn't prevent herself from reacting to him, then she would make sure that no part of her anatomy touched his. "What are you doing?"

"Taking the next sheet. I can probably raise the number from the impression left."

"What shall I do now?" Marie asked.

"I'll take the desk while you work on that locked credenza," Lucas instructed in a low voice. "Keep one eye on the door. Nash didn't impress me as a fool." He handed her his penlight and another appeared from his back pocket.

Marie managed to spring the lock to the credenza without doing any damage. She concentrated on being as quiet as possible as she swung open the veneered door and reached for the first drawer. The metal squeal it made stopped her. She wasn't sure if it was really loud, or if the sound was magnified by her knowledge that they could both go to jail if they were caught.

She felt Lucas's eyes boring into her. She wanted to tell him that the noise hadn't been her fault, but they had agreed to keep conversation to an absolute minimum.

The first drawer contained what looked like information on the various courses offered. The divider tabs had titles like Ten Steps To A Better Marriage and Living In Harmony As A Couple. If circumstances had been different, she might have grabbed the one on harmonious living. Lord knew, she and Lucas could use a little harmony.

Why? her brain screamed. It wasn't as though they were going to stay together.

Marie adjusted the penlight in her hand and forced herself to concentrate. All of her muscles were tense as she rummaged through the top and then the bottom drawer, scanning the different pages. Whoever set up the filing system had been accurate. Nothing seemed out of the ordinary, so she moved on to the right side of the credenza after briefly listening for any signs that they had been discovered.

If Lucas was having any better luck, he didn't let on. Marie continued her task in silence. The first drawer was more of the same—articles and reference materials. The bottom drawer was a different story. She bit back her excitement as she began reading the client contracts for the previous year.

She recognized David's fluid handwriting immediately. He had kept copious notes on all the couples who had come through Haven. Marie's eyes grew wide as she read file after file through the first half of the year. Then it appeared that David stopped taking notes. Or maybe the notes were now filed elsewhere in the office. At any rate, a seed had been planted in her mind.

She was about to turn and share her good news with Lucas when the lights flickered on. Lucas leaped over the chair, instantly putting his body between her and the small pistol pointed in their general direction.

"The gun isn't necessary, Nash," she heard Lucas say. "We can talk about this."

Marie realized that Lucas was attempting to pass her something. With an economy of motion, she took the papers from his hand, folded them and worked them down the front of her slip. All the while Lucas kept Nash talking. She tapped his back once as a signal when the papers were securely hidden.

"I'd like to know what you hoped to gain by riffling through confidential materials," Graham said. "As a doctor, you could lose your license for this."

Marie felt her heart fall to her feet. She had considered the possibility that they could go to jail if they were caught. The further risk Lucas was taking had never once played in her thoughts.

"It was my idea," she said, stepping to the side. "I insisted that Lucas come with me. I'm the one who picked the locks. He's not guilty of anything other than being in the same room with me. Please let Lucas go. He won't tell anyone what you've done."

Graham looked perplexed. "What I've done?"

"Please?" Marie pleaded. "I'm sure you had good reason to kill David. It—"

"Me?" he asked with apparent amazement. "I loved David as if we were brothers."

"Then, why did you lie?" Lucas demanded.

Graham's eyes flickered with an emotion Marie hoped was indecision. "Please, Dr. Nash. If you know anything that can help me, please tell me. I don't want to spend the rest of my life in prison for a murder I didn't commit."

Slowly, he lowered the pistol. Marie let out the breath she'd been holding.

"Sit down," Graham instructed. "I have to think about this."

He went behind the desk, closing the drawers before he sat down across from them. Lucas didn't take a chair. Instead, he stood at her side with one hand gripping her shoulder. Marie could tell by his stance that he was coiled, ready to spring if the other man made a threatening move.

Graham rubbed his red-tinged eyes and let out an audible breath. "I find it very curious that *you* would break into my office and accuse *me* of murder."

"You told us David had stopped coming here,"

Lucas said. "We have hard evidence that he was telling the IRS another story."

When Graham put the revolver inside his desk, Marie sighed her relief. If ever a man looked torn, it was Graham Nash. His eyes were troubled, and he seemed to have lost his usual exuberance. He looked directly at Marie. "If you did kill David, it wouldn't make much sense for you to break in here."

"I didn't kill him," Marie said. "But someone who knew David and me is trying really hard to make it look like I did."

Graham was pensive. "Could this have something to do with the fact that you pretended to be involved with David?"

"Excuse me?" Marie said.

"David told me all about it."

"He didn't tell me," Marie said. "What are you talking about?"

"David carried a photograph of you in his wallet. He showed it to me once and said you were the perfect cover."

"Cover for what?" Lucas asked.

"I don't know, David wouldn't say. I thought it might have something to do with money. Blackmail, perhaps?"

The last comment was directed at Marie. "I don't need to resort to blackmail," she insisted. "I'm far from destitute."

"Back up," Lucas said. "Why did you think it was about money?"

"David started having problems about eighteen months ago," Graham said.

"What kind of troubles?"

The psychiatrist sighed. "He didn't say. In fact, he denied there was anything wrong."

"Did you believe him?"

"I knew David well. He started neglecting his patients. It didn't take long before I was handling most of the work."

"What about his practice back in New Orleans?" Lucas asked.

"I was covering some of his cases. He referred a lot of his longtime patients to other doctors."

"How do you know that?" Marie asked.

"Requests for medical records."

"David never offered any explanation?"

Nash shook his head. "No. At first I thought he might have a problem with drugs or alcohol."

"Why?"

"Because of the money."

"What about the money?" Lucas probed.

"Haven Cottages was set up to be self-supporting and with an eye toward future expansion. About a year ago, David started making regular withdrawals from our capital improvements account."

"How regular?" Marie asked.

"Monthly, sometimes twice a month."

She didn't bother to hide her excitement. The blackmail theory seemed the most likely.

Lucas gave her shoulder a gentle squeeze before he asked, "How much was he taking?"

"A couple thousand at a time. It wasn't a problem at first."

"Then what happened?"

Graham shook his head dejectedly. "The account

ran dry about three months ago. I hoped that would bring David back into the practice.''

"But he sold his interest instead," Lucas supplied.

Nash eyed him warily. "Yes."

"He didn't give any explanation or warning?"

"No." Graham rubbed his tired eyes. "If you were willing to do all this just to get into my files, you must really be desperate to clear yourself, Mrs. Henderson. I hope you won't do it at the expense of David's reputation and memory. He was a fine man."

"I won't," Marie promised. "Unless I have no other choice."

"I kept hoping that he would come around eventually. Now he won't have the chance." He lowered his head to his hands and was silent for several long moments.

"Can we leave?" Marie asked quietly.

"Yes."

She reached over and touched his sleeve. "I don't know how to thank you."

Graham offered a weak smile. "Find the person that killed my friend. Then I'll know I did the right thing by letting you leave here tonight."

Lucas didn't drop her hand even after they were clear of the office building. The pathway to their cabin was well lit, but there was no sound except for the gentle rustling of the trees.

Marie struggled to keep pace with the tall man at her side. "Slow down," she urged.

"Sorry," he whispered, letting her hand slip away from his. "I forget how small you are."

"It's you who are tall," Marie retorted.

As soon as they walked into the cabin, Lucas

started throwing things into his suitcase. "Hurry up and pack," he instructed.

Marie retrieved the papers from their hiding place in her slip. "What are these?"

Lucas took them from her before she had a chance to examine them. "We can worry about them later. For now, we'd better get moving. I don't want Nash to have second thoughts and call the cops."

Marie followed his lead and packed with haste. "I think he believed me," she mused. "I don't think he's the killer. He seemed too sincere."

They were on the nearly deserted road back to New Orleans in less than thirty minutes. "Do you have any idea what he was talking about when he said you were a cover?"

Marie brought her hand to her mouth to stifle a yawn. The adrenaline had dissipated by now and she suddenly felt tired. "Maybe David was gay."

Lucas gave a low, throaty chuckle. "I saw the guy in action during our younger days. He definitely wasn't gay."

Marie sank further back into the seat. "Then why else would he need a cover?"

"To make another man jealous?" Lucas suggested.

"Or another woman as you said before."

Marie closed her eyes and let the hum of the engine lull her to sleep. When she opened her eyes, she discovered they were parked in front of his condo. "That didn't take long," she said.

"You weren't driving," he teased as he placed a kiss on her forehead. "It's good to be home."

Home. His home. She was only there on a temporary visa. She couldn't lose sight of that. Not if she was going to walk away from this with only her heart shattered.

Lucas barely spoke as they rode the elevator up to his apartment. Marie assumed he was merely tired, but they were barely through the door when he unfolded the letter he'd stolen from the Haven offices and handed it to her.

Lucas watched intently as Marie sat down on the sofa and opened the note. Her expression didn't falter when she read the words that were still etched in his brain.

After she was finished, she lifted her face and met his eyes. She didn't say anything. No explanation, nothing.

"Care to tell me about that?" he said, jamming his hands in his pockets.

And then she smiled. It wasn't an expression of joy. No, it was the same smile he'd seen when she'd been at her sister's bedside. It was so sad, so forced that it inspired compassion, an emotion he didn't want to feel right now. Not when he knew they were getting close to the end. When she would walk out of his life forever.

"You're amused?" he asked incredulously. "You should be grateful. If the cops ever get hold of that, you'll go to jail for sure."

"You really think I wrote this?"

Lucas made a guttural sound. "What am I supposed to think, Marie? It's signed by you."

"The note is typewritten," she began, rising from the sofa in a graceful, fluid motion. "The only signature is the letter *M*. And just for the record," she continued, coming right up close to him and looking directly into his face, "you can be *very* stupid at times."

She seemed so believable, but he wanted to hear her say the words. He had to know. "This note isn't from you to David? Those aren't your declarations of love?" He couldn't bring himself to ask about the rest of the note's contents. The mere thought that she had shared with David the same passion she had with him left Lucas feeling raw.

She met his eyes. "I was never in love with David, and apparently he was only using me for some reason I still don't understand. If you think I would lie to you, then I don't know you any better than I thought I knew him."

"I want to believe you, but first I find the picture and now this."

Marie brushed past him and went to the window. Her spine was straight as she turned her back to him. "I won't explain that picture to you again. Either you believe me or you don't. Your choice."

Lucas didn't say a word. To Marie, his silence was nothing short of an accusation. The hurt that gripped her was almost unbearable. She lifted a steady hand to the curtains and parted them. The sun was just beginning to paint the sky a warm pink. "David referred people to my shop. I thought it was because we were friends. Thanks to David, the opening of Heaven Scent was packed. I made enough money that day to make a go of the business. I thought he did that because of friendship. I guess I'm not very adept at deciphering people's true motives, huh?"

Balling his hands into fists, Lucas tried to think of the best way to apologize. He doubted anything short of throwing himself out the window could make up for his inexcusable behavior. Why did this little wisp of a woman have him so off balance?

He walked up behind her and placed his hands at her waist. "Marie?" he began. "I'm really—"

"Please don't," she said in a voice he had never before heard and hoped he would never hear in the future. It was too full of pain and hurt. Pain and hurt that were his doing.

"Finding that note really threw me," he explained. If only she would turn around. "I guess I jumped to the wrong conclusion yet again."

"And what do you expect me to say to that?" The words came out in a flat monotone.

Lucas started to touch her again but stopped his hand in midair. "I'll tell you what I want."

Marie turned and faced him. Her face was blank. The spirit was gone from her eyes. It was as though he had extinguished her fire from the inside out. "What you want doesn't matter to me in the least."

He flinched as if she had struck him. "I made a mistake," he explained. "I can only apologize."

"Thank you."

There was no feeling behind those words. Either she didn't believe he was genuinely sorry or she didn't care. Judging by her vacant expression, he guessed the latter was more accurate.

"What can I do to prove to you that I'm truly sorry for acting like such a jerk?"

She didn't move a muscle. There was no reaction at all as he tried to coax a smile from her. It was almost scary. "You don't need to do anything, Lucas.

I can see how you could have gotten the impression that I had been the one to send David that note.''

"Good," he breathed. His enthusiasm didn't last. Not when he saw her eyeing him with unabashed loathing. "I saw the signature and I overreacted."

"There isn't any need to belabor the point," she told him. "Is there anything else you'd like me to explain before I leave?"

"Leave?"

"I assume that would be for the best. We obviously can't continue with this farce. I'll just—"

"We made a deal, Marie. We're married until the end of the trial. You gave me your word."

"Suit yourself."

There was no fight in her. Nothing but the stoic grace that took her from the room.

If he could have punched himself, he would have. He had never intentionally hurt a woman in his life. *And when he finally did, the woman was his wife*. He had to think. What could he do to convince her that he was sorry?

Lucas stuffed his hand in his pocket and took out the slip of paper from the pad on Nash's desk. After getting a pencil, he carefully rubbed the lead across the page until the image appeared. He recognized the number, all right, but he tried it just to be sure.

The phone was answered on the third ring by a familiar groggy voice.

"Carl Lee Shivley here."

CHAPTER SIXTEEN

"WHAT ARE YOU DOING?" Lucas asked her when he reappeared from the bedroom.

"I'm making a list."

He came around the desk and leaned over her shoulder. The feel of his warm body pressed against her chipped away at the wall of aloofness she had raised to protect herself. The hurt had evolved into a dull ache during the hour they'd spent in separate parts of the condo.

"Let me help you."

"No."

"Why not? We're supposed to be in this together."

She didn't want him to be nice. His reaction to the note had been a brutal awakening. Not only did Lucas not respect her, he also still didn't trust her. That much was painfully, obviously clear.

"The only thing we do together with any amount of success is have sex," she answered honestly.

"Marie." He said her name so softly that it almost sounded reverent.

She wouldn't look at him. She couldn't. Lucas's ability to wear her down was too dangerous. Especially if she was going to get out of this mess with some semblance of dignity. "I agree that we're stuck together. If we separate before the trial, we could face charges of fraud or hindering prosecution as well as a lot of embarrassing questions. It could cost you your career and I don't want that.''

"Thank you.''

She didn't want his gratitude. "But that doesn't mean I am willing to completely destroy my life.''

"I won't hurt you,'' he soothed, his large hand closing on her shoulder.

It's too late, she thought, remaining rigid under the weight of her resolve. "We won't hurt each other anymore. We're intelligent adults.''

"Agreed.''

"Which means we should be able to get through this for the short time we'll be together.''

"Marie?''

He did it again. There was an almost magnetic pull to the way he said her name. She closed her eyes and prayed for strength. Strength was the only weapon she had left.

"You made a huge sacrifice for me and I'll always be grateful,'' she said.

"But?''

"I also realize that for some perverse reason, we have this undeniable chemistry between us.''

Lucas's only response was to run the pad of his thumb along her cheek. All she had to do was tilt her head and she could be in his arms again. Her body ached to do just that. Her heart ached knowing she didn't dare.

"We will both be better off in the long run if we ignore the chemistry.'' Her voice was clipped and cool. "We aren't teenagers and we should be able to control ourselves for the short time we have left.''

Lucas's sweet touch fell away. "Is that really what you want?"

He sounded disappointed. But then, why wouldn't he? She hadn't exactly made a habit of telling him no in the past.

"It is."

He sighed loudly before she felt the weight of his body lift from her. His sense of honor would prevent him from going against her wishes, she knew that. Just as she knew it would take a lifetime to forget what they had experienced between them. But she had to. She didn't have a choice.

Lucas went into the kitchen and returned a few minutes later with two mugs of coffee. He placed one in front of her, then twisted the sheet in front of her so that he could read her notes.

"Who are these people?"

"Couples that David counseled at Haven."

"Why are you writing their names?"

Marie looked up from her work. He seemed to be taking her new definition of their relationship in stride. That spoke volumes about his feelings, or more accurately, lack thereof. If any part of her had held on to the foolish hope that he regarded her with affection, it was instantly dispelled. *Just as well*, she thought with a sigh.

"Whoever killed David also knew that I was treating him."

Lucas nodded. His hair was still damp, and she found it impossible to speak as she watched a droplet of water make a sensual path down the side of his face.

"When I was going through his records last night,

I realized that David used to send people to me on a fairly regular basis.''

"And you think one of them might have something to do with the murder.''

"It's worth a try. I'm betting my freedom on the idea that David had a woman in his life. A woman who was very important to him.''

Lucas seemed suddenly agitated and he would no longer meet her eyes. He probably didn't think her theory was valid.

"I'm going to make a list and take it to Desiree.''

"What for?''

"Because I don't have all the receipts. I need to use her sight to see if I can figure out who *M* is.''

"That's a good idea.''

Marie gaped at him. "Excuse me?''

He shrugged and offered a small grin. "I'm not willing to convert to voodoo, but if Desiree can help, go for it.''

"You are full of surprises," she muttered, turning back to her list.

"I'm not finished yet," he said softly. "That note didn't look recent. David might not have been still seeing his mystery woman when he was killed.''

"I still have to try. It's not as if I have a lot of other leads to go on.''

"We might have one," Lucas said.

Marie's head came up with a snap. "What?''

"I was able to pull up the impression of the phone number from the note.''

Marie felt her spirits brighten. "And?''

"It's the private, unlisted home number of my boss.''

"Carl Lee?" Marie didn't hide her surprise. "Why would Graham Nash have Carl Lee's number?"

"I'm on my way to ask him."

Marie scrambled to her feet. "I'm coming."

Lucas placed his hands on her shoulders and held her gaze. "No. Let me handle this alone."

"Why?"

He tapped the tip of her nose with his index finger. "You aren't the only one who's been thinking. Carl Lee fought me over the autopsy results."

"You think he was in a hurry to see me take the blame?"

A flash of pain clouded his eyes. "I wish I had followed my gut on this. I never should have listened to Carl Lee when we got the preliminary results back. If I had handled it differently—gone more slowly— maybe you wouldn't be in this position right now."

Marie offered him a half smile. "I'm hoping to look back on this when I'm eighty and laugh."

"I hope we both will," he said, and the pain seemed to dissipate. He grew more animated. "Carl Lee would have no trouble finding out what you were doing. He's lived here his whole life, and the two of you probably know all the same people."

"I can't see Carl Lee letting me go to jail. He took my tonsils out when I was a kid."

"Carl Lee said some pretty unkind things about your family. I think he's suffering from a severe case of Delacroix envy. And if my hunch is right, it could be that Carl Lee wasn't acting alone."

"You think someone else from the hospital might be involved?"

"I don't know. But Carl Lee didn't seem overly

concerned when I told him about Shelby and Joanna being run off the road.''

Marie placed her hand over her rapidly beating heart. "Carl Lee could have killed them."

"Or the redhead."

"Shelby's trying to get her name now."

"My guess is she'll lead back to Carl Lee."

"But why?"

"That's what I want to know," Lucas said with steel in his voice.

"Let me come with you," she fairly begged. "It's my life he's been jerking around. Not to mention my sister, my cousin and poor David."

"I want you to stay here. Don't open the door for anyone but me."

"Why?"

Lucas took her hand and brought it to his lips. Opening her fingers, he brushed her palm with his lips. "If I'm right, Marie, someone is trying to hurt you. I don't want that to happen. I couldn't—"

"Okay," she agreed quickly. It was the only way she could think to get her hand away from the searing heat of his lips. "But please call me as soon as you know anything."

"I will. Promise."

DESIREE WAS ON HER PORCH with a shotgun cradled under her arm when Marie stepped from the boat. Despite her assurance to Lucas she had rented a car and raced for the swamp as soon as he had left the building.

The older woman's expression was solemn as she greeted Marie with a hug.

"He chased you back here, *non?*" Desiree asked.

Marie nodded. "I really need your help. Somehow everything got all screwed up and I don't know what to do. I just know I don't have much time."

"That's true enough," Desiree agreed. "Did you bring the card?"

She nodded and they went inside. Marie fell into a chair and let her handbag drop to the floor of the shack with a thud. The pungent scent of oils and herbs filled the air. "Do you know if Carl Lee knows anything about the cards?"

Desiree's brow wrinkled as she returned from the cabinet holding her velvet pouch of bones. "Not by me," she answered. "Why this sudden interest in old Carl Lee?"

"He's involved in David's murder," Marie explained. "We found evidence when we were up north."

"Things aren't always so easy. Why isn't Lucas with you? I told you to stay close to him. That man is your future, Marie. I saw it as clearly as I'm seeing you now."

"I know," Marie breathed. "I tried. It just didn't work out like I thought. Maybe what you saw has another meaning, since Lucas and I don't have a future."

"Why not? You love the man."

Marie's chest grew heavy. "When I decided not to go to medical school, do you remember what you told me?"

Desiree smiled. "Your daddy was giving you the devil."

"And you told me to demand respect. I did."

"I told you to demand respect and to make sure you gave it," she corrected her gently. "What does this have to do with your young man?"

"Lucas doesn't respect me. He thinks aromatherapy is a joke. He thinks I'm a joke."

"Has he said this?"

"Well...not in so many words."

"Have you asked him how he feels?"

Marie colored. "I don't have to. Besides, I don't think I could stand to hear him say it."

"Maybe you would be surprised by his answers."

"He doesn't trust me or respect me. How could I fall in love with a man like that? I should have known better."

"The heart and the mind don't always work in harmony," Desiree said. "Give it time." She became pensive, making no move to scatter the bones she used to concentrate. Marie knew better than to tell the woman to hurry along. Desiree believed there was an appropriate time for all things. She didn't acknowledge time the way most people did. This was one instance when Marie wished that wasn't the case.

Desiree met Marie's eyes. "You belong to him now."

"Not really," Marie admitted. "I thought I could...that if we... He doesn't love me."

The woman snorted. "Doesn't he understand destiny?"

"No. He'll walk out of my life as soon as the trial is over."

"No trial." Desiree was adamant. She spilled the bones onto the tray and ran her fingers over them.

Her eyes rolled back as Marie waited, kept company by the silence and her own anxiety.

"You will know how he feels when you take off that ring that he gave you."

Marie glanced down at her hand. The expensive band seemed a part of her now. Just as Lucas was a part of her heart.

"I don't understand," she said. "Once Lucas uncovers why Carl Lee had David killed, it will be over. For all I know, it's already happened."

"No," Desiree cried, her expression pained. "There's colors. Brown. No, beige."

"Beige?" Marie repeated. "What's beige, Desiree?"

"*Je ne sais pas.* But only Lucas can keep you from harm, and you him."

"Lucas isn't stupid. He went to see Carl Lee at the hospital. Carl Lee wouldn't dare do anything to him there."

"*Non!*" Desiree insisted, her expression becoming more intense. "You are not safe. You will smell the bud of the rose."

On the trip back to Lucas's condo, Marie racked her brain trying to decipher Desiree's meaning. She attempted to piece all the images into a coherent idea. But the color beige, the scent of roses and her wedding ring didn't have a common thread that she could grasp.

"Rose," she murmured as she hit the first pocket of traffic. "Rose is one of the true essential oils. I don't use it often...." Suddenly, her mind homed in on a single thought. "But I *sell* a lot of it."

IGNORING THE HORN from the car behind her, Marie made an illegal turn and gunned the midsize car down toward the Quarter. "Someone who bought rose oil from me in the past," she repeated like a mantra until she pulled into the alley behind her building. Abandoning the car, she quickly unlocked the door and was inside the store, her heart pounding in her ears.

Flipping on lights as she went, Marie passed through the therapy room and into the front of the shop. Her purse fell to the floor as she tossed her keys on the glass counter and reached beneath the register for her cash receipt books.

"Okay," she whispered, tucking a lock of hair behind her ear. "Rose oil is stock number..."

Cursing softly, she reached behind her and grabbed a bottle of rose oil from the shelf. After committing the number to memory, she took the first invoice and started her search.

Her initial excitement began to fade. She had sold a great deal of rose oil, but there didn't seem to be any pattern to the sales. Some weeks she had sold twenty bottles. One month she had sold only one to her longtime customer, Ken Rogers.

Dejectedly, she returned the books to their place and reached again for one of the bottles of rose oil. "No beige on the label," she whispered.

The sound of the phone disrupted her thoughts. While still holding the small bottle in her hand, she lifted the receiver with the other and said, "Heaven Scent, may I help you?"

She could hear static, but little else. "Hello?" she called in a stronger voice.

She didn't know if she got a response or not. She

dropped the phone and screamed as gunshots shattered the front window, and then the countertop exploded before her.

CHAPTER SEVENTEEN

CARL LEE WAS IN his office when Lucas barged in. The rotund man looked shocked. "Something I can do for you, son?"

Lucas wanted to jump over the desk and pummel the man. He settled for leaning forward, his fingertips resting on the desktop. He stared right into Carl Lee's eyes and demanded, "What do you know about Haven Cottages?"

"What business is it of yours?" Carl Lee answered in a neutral tone.

"I want to know why Graham Nash had your unlisted number on his desk."

It didn't take long for perspiration to bring a slight sheen to Carl Lee's upper lip. "What did he say?"

Lucas took his best shot and prayed the gamble would pay off. "He told me you were the one who bought David's share. You set up some dummy corporation to hide what you were doing."

Carl Lee lost the game of chicken by shrugging his shoulders. "So what?"

"So why didn't you tell me that when David's body was brought in?"

Carl Lee removed a handkerchief from his jacket pocket and wiped his brow. "I didn't think it was relevant."

"Did you feel that way when you gave that reporter the picture of Marie and David? Did you bother to tell him that you had business dealings with the deceased?"

Something very close to a sneer tugged at Carl Lee's mouth. "So this is all about your *wife?*"

"Careful," Lucas warned.

"She shakes her tail feathers and you blow a pretty decent bit of forensic work. I hope it's worth it, son."

Lucas reached across the desk and caught Carl Lee by the tie. He lifted him out of his seat. "Make one more remark about my wife and you'll be picking your teeth out of your coffee."

"I can have you arrested," Carl Lee gasped. "I could probably have you committed, too."

"From your prison cell?"

"I don't know what that woman's done to your brain, son. But you're way off base here."

"Then, explain things to me," Lucas said, releasing the man with a shove.

Carl Lee regained his balance and straightened in his chair. If he was the least bit intimidated, he sure didn't show it. "Dr. Markum came to me about six months ago and offered to sell me his interest in Haven."

"Why you?"

"I sent some business his way about a year-and-a-half back. I just assumed he was returning the favor."

"What kind of business?"

"I had a patient who had a bad marriage. I knew Markum by reputation, so I sent her to him."

"A redhead?" Lucas asked.

Carl Lee looked puzzled and shook his head. "Amanda Rossner is a brunette. I asked Markum about her when he brought me the deal. He said he'd convinced her to leave her husband."

"David was in the business of saving marriages," Lucas said.

"And I had set Amanda's arm twice and wrapped her cracked ribs three times in less than five years. How many times do you think a healthy twenty-five-year-old can fall down the stairs or blacken her eye by running into a door?"

"Abuse?"

Carl Lee shrugged. "She never would admit it to me. I wanted to send her to the D.A. to have her husband arrested but I had to settle for sending her to counseling."

"That's your only connection to David?"

"Yes."

"Then why did you go to such elaborate lengths to hide your purchase of David's interest?"

"This is the South, son. It would only take one Bible-toting fanatic to destroy my political career. Haven isn't exactly what you might call a run-of-the-mill operation. It has gotten some pretty bad press a few times. When it first opened, a lot of folks in these parts believed it was part nudist colony and part sex spa."

Raking his hands through his hair, Lucas took a deep breath. "I guess I owe you an apology."

"I guess you do," Carl Lee agreed, just as his secretary stuck her head in the office. "What is it?"

"I'm sorry, but I just took a call from the hospital operator."

"Yes?" Carl Lee prodded impatiently.

"It was concerning Dr. Henderson's wife."

Lucas spun and met the woman's sympathetic eyes. "Marie?"

"I'm sorry to be the one to have to tell you this. You two being newly married and all—"

"What?" Lucas thundered.

"An ambulance was dispatched to Mrs. Henderson's store about twenty minutes ago."

Lucas felt the room spin as he listened to the woman. Somehow he knew it was bad. "What was the call for?" he asked.

"Shots fired with injury."

"ARE YOU ALL RIGHT?" Lucas asked after he had shoved his way through to the back of the ambulance where Marie sat.

Dropping his medical bag, he cupped her face. The fear in her eyes stabbed him in the gut. Ignoring the technician, who pronounced her fine except for the gash on her hand, Lucas did his own evaluation. He found nothing except a rather nasty cut on her palm that needed stitches.

"I'm okay," she said weakly. "It scared me more than anything else."

He carefully rebandaged her hand and placed it against her body before he helped her to stand on shaky legs. Retrieving his bag, he led Marie out of the ambulance.

"She needs stitches!" the ambulance attendant called.

"I'll take care of it," Lucas called back.

A gruff-looking patrolman stood guarding the entrance to the shop. "You can't come in here."

"Look—I'm Dr. Henderson and this is my wife. I'm going to take her upstairs to see to her injury." Lucas lifted her against him when he heard her let out a small sound. He cradled her head, careful not to disturb her injured hand. With his other hand, he supported her beneath the knees, his medical bag dangling from his fingers.

"I guess it will be okay." The police officer sounded reluctant. "We're just waiting for the crime scene guys."

The shop looked as if a bomb had gone off inside it. Lucas shuddered to think of Marie amid this near-total destruction. It was hard to find a spot that wasn't sprayed with shotgun pellets. It was also hard to breathe and walk. The floor was slippery and very pungent now. Oil ran in small streams and pooled amid the broken bottles. Brightly colored candles rolled on the floor, resting against the mounds of incense that had spilled from shattered tins. He didn't think there was a single thing in the shop that had been saved. Except, thank heavens, Marie.

"You can put me down," she said as he climbed the backstairs two at a time. "I hadn't realized how bad it was until we walked back inside."

"What happened?" Lucas asked, using his foot to open the door to her apartment. He placed Marie on the sofa, set his bag down and went to the sink to wash his hands.

"The police think it was someone who simply doesn't want me in the neighborhood."

Glancing over his shoulder, he rolled his eyes to

indicate his take on that opinion. "I hope you set them straight."

"I tried, but when you're on bail for a manslaughter charge and you smell like a big room deodorizer, people don't tend to take you too seriously."

"I'm glad you still have your sense of humor. You're going to need it when I start stitching."

"What makes you think I'm going to watch?" she quipped. "And would you mind waiting until after you finish stitching my hand to ream me for not following your orders."

Tilting his head to one side, he regarded her pale face and the deep worry lines near her mouth and eyes. Her dress was stained with blood and oils. She was a sight. But she was alive and well, save the minor injury to her palm. Reaching into his bag, Lucas pulled out some gloves and snapped them over his hands. When he looked at Marie again, she had gone an even lighter shade of pale.

"I'm really good at this," he assured her with a quick brush of his mouth against hers. "I'll even guarantee you won't have a scar."

"I'm a total wimp," she warned.

Lucas squeezed her knee as he pulled the syringe of topical anesthetic from his bag. "This might sting," he said. He took the suture kit from the bag and ripped it open with his teeth. "After that it will be smooth sailing. Okay?"

She didn't answer. She couldn't. She had fainted.

I SMELLED THE ROSES. And I saw...

"Welcome back," Lucas greeted when her eyes flew open. "You really *are* a wimp."

"My hand hurts," she said as she lifted it and looked at the fresh bandage.

"I can give you a shot for a painkiller or call in a prescription. Take your pick."

Marie used her good hand to scoot up into a sitting position. "I still reek of roses."

The minute she said the word, memories came to her in a flash of broken images.

Lucas touched his wrist to her forehead. "You look pale again. I cleaned the wound, but I'm still worried about infection. We'll stop on the way home and I'll get you some antibiotics."

Marie wasn't really listening to him. "Roses and beige," she muttered.

"What about them?"

"It won't be over until I find the connection."

Lucas was staring at her as if she had grown another head. "Maybe we should stop by the ER. A laceration doesn't cause delirium."

"I'm not delirious," she insisted. Throwing her legs over the bed, she got up and walked to her closet. "I'm just thinking out loud—ouch!"

Lucas appeared at her side. "I didn't spend all that time doing perfectly spaced sutures just for you to destroy my work."

"I can't undo my dress with only one hand," she confessed, feeling her face warm with color. "Mind helping me get out of this thing?"

His eyes darkened, and she noticed that a tiny vein stood out near his temple. "What are you planning to do?"

"Nothing dangerous. I just need a quick shower. I

smell like a florist's shop and there's blood all over me.''

Lucas's mouth twitched with amusement. "Is vanity a mortal or a venial sin?''

Marie returned his smile. "Neither. Cleanliness is next to godliness. I have a priest in my family, remember?''

"You win,'' he replied.

"I want that one.'' She indicated the dress to Lucas. "And I'll need a slip and...other things from the dresser.'' Why did she feel so awkward, she wondered, annoyed at herself. Lucas was hardly a stranger. She felt him following her toward the dresser and stopped suddenly, intending to tell him she was capable of showering on her own.

The sudden halt nearly caused a collision. Instinctively, Marie raised her uninjured palm and placed it against Lucas's solid chest. Through the soft fabric of his shirt she felt the solid definition of his muscles. She swallowed—hard. Apparently her little fainting spell hadn't dulled the portion of her brain that controlled sexual awareness. In fact, it seemed to have sharpened it.

Her eyes traveled from the back of her hand up to his eyes. She experienced a sensation much like dizziness when she met his intense gaze. She tilted her head back and his breath washed over her upturned face in warm, comforting waves. Marie could feel the rhythm of his heart beating beneath her hand. It was as quick and uneven as her own.

"You don't need to follow me around. I'm just going to clean up and change out of these disgusting clothes.'' Having said that, she took a step backward.

Lucas allowed the hanger holding the dress she'd chosen to dangle from one long finger. "I'm worried about you. You had quite a shock today, and I don't think it would be wise to leave you alone for the next few hours."

Marie gave him a patient look. "I appreciate the free medical care, but I'm fine. I'm certainly capable of taking a shower."

He sighed heavily and shook his head. "I think we've reached an impasse here, so I'm going to suggest a compromise."

"Compromise?" she mocked playfully. "I didn't think you knew the meaning of that word."

Lucas reached down and stroked her cheek. "I'm just being nice because you're injured. When you're back in top form, all bets are off."

"What kind of compromise?"

"A shower is out of the question."

"But—"

"But a bath is okay, so long as you don't get the stitches wet."

Marie nodded. "It's a deal."

"I'll wash your hair for you. It's too long for you to manage by yourself."

Marie hesitated a moment, then nodded her head. "What would be the easiest way for us to do this?"

"Just take off all your clothes and I'll handle the rest." He grinned at her lasciviously.

Marie counted to ten, then twenty. It took her the count of thirty-five before she regained her patience. "Don't you feel just a *little* guilty for coming on to me when I've been shot at, cut up and sewn back together? Not to mention passing out and possibly fighting an infection?''

Lucas tossed the clean dress on the bed and stepped forward. He was close enough that she could feel the rough fabric of his jeans against her thighs. ''It was a joke, Marie. Not a pass.'' His voice was deep and incredibly sexy. ''If I ever make a pass at you again, you'll know it.''

His words tingled in her ears, matching the sensations deep in the pit of her stomach. ''Thanks for the warning,'' she joked, hoping to inject a little lightness into the mood.

Lucas helped her layer the floor of her bathroom with towels before she knelt down and leaned over, using her good hand to flip her matted and oily hair into the tub.

With incredible care, Lucas lathered and rinsed the dark tresses. Normally she considered having her hair shampooed a treat, but this was something completely different. His hands deftly kneaded her scalp in sensual, circular motions that left her reeling. Her awareness of this man had reached a new and frightening level.

''All done,'' he announced, once he had rinsed all the shampoo from her hair. ''I'll go see if the police still want to talk to you when you're ready. Can I help you get out of your dress first?''

''No!'' she answered quickly, too quickly. Lightening her tone, she added, ''Thanks, anyway.''

When the door closed and she was finally alone, Marie let out a long-held breath. ''Be still my heart,'' she whispered as she tried, unsuccessfully, to unbutton her now damp dress. Frustrated in every sense of the word, she grabbed one side of the dress and gave a good yank. The buttons scattered all across the floor, the dress went into the trash, and her body went into the warm water with the hopes that she could restore her equilibrium before he returned.

"MARIE?"

"In here!"

Lucas went to the still closed bathroom door and knocked softly. "The police want to take your statement. How much longer do you think you'll be?"

"When do these cursed stitches come out?"

"Is something wrong?"

"You could say that."

He pushed open the door and found her near tears. "Are you dizzy? Nauseous?"

"I'm half-naked!" she snapped.

Lucas felt a part of his body relax. She was okay. But then other parts of his anatomy tensed as his gaze roamed over her. Her hair was a mass of glistening ringlets, framing her flushed face. She had managed to get into the undergarments he had left for her without any apparent difficulty. The delicate pattern of the black satin-and-lace bra was visible to him, as was a hint of the matching panties. He didn't think she would like it if she knew how thoroughly he had enjoyed making the selection.

"I can't get the buttons done up on this dress."

Lucas erased all expression from his face before stepping to her aid. He worked quickly, trying not to think about how warm her skin felt when he brushed it with the backs of his hand. He forced himself to concentrate on helping her into the dress—anything other than the way her breasts rose and fell with each slightly ragged breath. He was resolute in his desire not to embarrass them both by telling her what seeing just a glimpse of her perfect body did to him. He was in real trouble.

"All set," he said, pleased that his voice didn't betray the fact that his jeans were now at least two sizes too small.

"Thanks," she said.

Unexpectedly, she rose on tiptoe to place a kiss on his cheek. Lucas swallowed and left to get the waiting officer. The kiss she gave him had been nice. But he wasn't interested in nice. Not with the sight of her still etched in his brain.

He went down into what was left of the shop and found Officer Lawson. By the time the two men went upstairs to the apartment, Marie was in the process of making tea.

Lawson went directly to the sofa and sat down. "Have you ever had a problem with vandalism before?" he asked Marie.

"Vandalism?" she repeated, and Lucas heard the incredulity underlying the single word.

"The first floor is trashed," Lawson commented. "Any idea who might want to do something like that?"

"The same person who framed me for the murder of David Markum?" she suggested.

Lawson looked disinterested, but then he probably heard cries of "frame-up" on a daily basis. "Do you know anyone who drives an old four-door?" He paused and flipped back in his notes. "Tan, beige or maybe cream-colored?"

"No," Marie answered. "Why?"

"We found a street performer who thinks the shots came from a car fitting that description."

"Was it an old gas guzzler with rusted-out fenders?" Lucas asked.

Lawson pushed his hat back off his forehead. "Why?"

Lucas shrugged. "I thought I might have seen a car like that around here a couple of weeks back."

"Did you happen to see the plate?" Lawson asked.

"Sorry."

The rest of the interview consisted of Lawson taking down the address of Lucas's condo and explaining that these types of random crime were almost impossible to solve. He also suggested that Marie should be thrilled that nothing more than her shop was riddled with buckshot. It was the only thing the two men agreed on.

"We're getting out of here," Lucas said as soon as the officer had left. "This was about as random as the Fourth of July."

Marie was smiling.

"What?"

"The beige."

"The beige *what?*"

CHAPTER EIGHTEEN

"WHY DIDN'T YOU LIGHT into me earlier?" she asked after they had detoured to a pharmacy, where Lucas had made arrangements for an antibiotic and a pain-killer. Marie had insisted on calling her family before they saw the evening news and thought the worst.

"I've learned that it doesn't accomplish much to trade insults," he said. "Especially with you."

"I guess not. The only thing we have in common is sex."

Lucas frowned. "Whatever gave you that idea?"

"Because it's the only time when we're together that I don't feel like I'm walking on eggshells. You have this uncanny ability to raise my stress level."

"And what cures stress?"

Marie blinked. Surely she hadn't heard him correctly. "Barbiturates, if I remember my pharmacology class."

He smiled at her. "I wasn't asking for the traditional method. I want to know what an aromatherapist would suggest."

She eyed him suspiciously. "Are you making fun of me?"

"I'm interested."

Marie glanced down at her hands. "Tangerine."

"Do you have any in that kit you carry around?"

She nodded.

Lucas went and retrieved the small amulet she indicated. After removing the stopper, he inhaled the fragrance. "This reminds me of spring break."

"Why?"

"We used to go to Florida for spring break, and the orange blossoms would be in bloom. It was a lot of fun."

Marie was wary. His abrupt change was confusing. "Why are you suddenly so interested in aromatherapy?"

He held the bottle out for her to smell. "Maybe I've decided that there might just be something to all this stuff. I liked your argument that if seeing was believing, smelling was, too. I also wanted you to realize that we have more in common than great sex."

Marie colored. "Such as?"

"We're both protective and loyal."

"So is a Doberman."

"We're also very passionate."

"Don't forget careless," she reminded him.

"That's part of the passion."

"Could we please change the subject?" Her mind simply couldn't absorb all this at one time. "Since you haven't said anything about Carl Lee, should I assume that he denied everything?"

"It was a dead end," he said. "I'll tell you all about it after I get those pills and some food into you."

"Don't you ever go off duty?"

"Not with you around," he teased, but then he seemed to read her uneasiness. "You don't have to look at me like that. I'm not offering you anything other than food and a decent night's sleep."

Marie should have been giddy with relief. Lucas was the absolute perfect gentleman. After she called her father, Lucas insisted that she sit at the table while he fixed her some soup, which he served to her along with two pills and a tall glass of water.

"I'll take these after you tell me what happened with Carl Lee."

Lucas shook his head. "You'll take them now or I won't tell you what I learned from Carl Lee."

"You're awfully pushy."

"Either take the pills or I'll have to switch to plan B."

"Plan B?"

"Plan B is where I get my medical bag and fill a syringe with—"

Marie raised her hand, then swallowed the pills with huge gulps of water. "A little juniper followed by some eucalyptus is a lot less toxic to the system," she grumbled.

"I'm sure it is, but you're going to humor me and take the full course of antibiotics. Don't make me get tough," he teased, sitting down beside her.

"It's a good thing you're a pathologist," Marie remarked, her eyelids drooping as the medication began to take effect. "You have absolutely no bedside manner."

Lucas pretended to be mortally wounded. "You shame me, woman!"

"Right…" She gave a huge yawn. "Sorry."

"No problem. Let's go sit on the sofa and I'll tell you all about my day."

That made her giggle. "You said that as if we were really married."

"You don't take medication very often, do you?"

"Nope. Why are you laughing?"

"Because you're funny."

Marie felt the soft cushions relax her even more. When Lucas joined her, she sighed and let her heavy head fall against his shoulder.

"Why don't you go to sleep? I can tell you—"

"No. I want you to tell me now."

"Carl Lee is only guilty of hiding behind a bogus corporation."

"*He's* the one who bought David's shares?"

"Yes. Why don't you tell me about the roses and the beige."

"I have to talk to Desiree." Even Marie could tell that her words were slurred. "I smelled the roses and I think the beige is the..."

"The beige *what?*"

"The beige," she whispered, just before her mind swirled down into the darkness.

WHEN MARIE OPENED her eyes again, the sun was already high in the sky. She bolted upright in the bed. Not *the* bed—*his* bed. Lifting the comforter, she gasped as a sharp pain shot through her left hand. She gasped again when she found herself wearing one of Lucas's shirts and nothing else. Rubbing one side of her face, she tried to remember what had happened. Surely they hadn't...

She tossed off the covers and padded out into the living room. "Lucas?"

Silence. She gave the room a quick survey, and

that's when she noticed the note propped against the pill bottles. The script was bold, masculine and just a little difficult to read. "Typical doctor," she muttered. "Take one of the blue pills with food," she read aloud. "There's coffee and tea in the kitchen. I got some—bagels, maybe?—at the store. Please rest. I have a meeting with my broker about David's finances. I'll be home before lunch. Lucas. P.S. No, we didn't."

She groaned as she tossed the note onto the table. "We didn't." With a sigh, she walked into the kitchen to put some water on to boil. "It's as if he can read my mind," she complained with a shiver. "I've got to talk to Desiree."

Marie twisted the wedding band on her finger. "Roses, beige and my ring. My ring off!" she cried. Why hadn't she thought of it before? She tugged at the band, but her fingers were still swollen from the injury to her hand. Ice didn't help and neither did butter. About the only thing she managed to do was make her hand throb and her puffy fingers greasy.

It took her quite a while to dress, but she managed to make herself presentable. *I'll leave him a note,* she thought, since he had extended that same courtesy to her. First she called a cab, then, going to the desk, she found a pad of paper. One name was written on it several times. "Amanda?" she said aloud.

Marie ripped off the top paper and wrote a note telling him she had gone to see Desiree and for him to meet her at the pier at lunchtime. She gave her word that she would wait for him there.

She had just finished when the security phone in the kitchen rang.

"Hello?"

"Your cab is here, Mrs. Henderson."

"I'll be right down," Marie told the concierge.

She emerged from the building and was met by an older gentleman with a warm smile. "Morning, ma'am. Dispatch said you wanted to go all the way out to Bayou Beltane?"

"Yes, please."

Marie delicately cradled her sore hand as the driver pulled away from the curb.

"Looks serious," he said on the breeze from his opened window.

"Not really," she returned conversationally. "I just cut myself on some glass."

"I hope it doesn't interfere with your plans for New Year's Eve."

"That's tomorrow, isn't it," she murmured.

"Me and the missus don't generally go out. My Mandy says that there's too many drunks on the road."

"Mandy?"

His reflection in the rearview mirror positively beamed. "My wife, Amanda. It will be forty-seven years come April."

"Mandy. Short for Amanda?"

"That's right."

Marie's thoughts went in a dozen different directions at once. "Um, I'm really sorry, but I've changed my mind. Can you drop me at the Quarter?"

"Is everything okay, miss? You seem upset."

"I'm fine. I just have to make an urgent call."

"You got it," he said kindly.

"Thanks," she said when they reached her shop. She paid the fare and gave the driver a generous tip.

"You sure you want to go in there?" he asked when he saw the police tape and boarded-up storefront.

"It isn't as bad as it looks," she assured him. "Thanks again."

Marie stepped through the maze of tape and boards. Lucas would probably be furious with her, but she would worry about that later. Acting on impulse had gotten her this far in life. Glass crunched beneath her shoes, and the lingering scent of the spilled oils almost caused her to choke.

"The phone," she whispered, cradling her sore arm and using one toe to kick through the mess. She found the cord. Then she found the phone—or what was left of it.

Swearing softly, she went through the back room to the stairs and up to her apartment. Because of her injury, she had to put her purse on the floor to dig out the keys. They weren't there.

"Improvise," she breathed, and took out a nail file and a hairpin. In a few short minutes she was inside. She picked up the phone and then set it down quickly, her shoulders slumped. Lucas had said he was at his broker's office. She had no idea how to contact him. Pager. She'd call the hospital and have him paged. Surely they would know where he was.

Lucas's secretary was on vacation. The fill-in didn't believe that she was actually his wife. "I'll be happy to hold while you check with Dr. Shivley," Marie said. "But this *is* an emergency."

"Please hold."

"Please hurry," she whispered.

A chill danced along her spine when she heard a thud from the floor below. Great, she thought. Looters or curiosity seekers. Just what I need. Marie listened distractedly to an instrumental adaptation of a heavy metal tune on the other end of the line. She heard another sound from the floor below. Impatience melded into uneasiness. Then she remembered that she had left the door to her apartment open.

Her heart raced when she heard what could have been someone on the backstairs. "Come on!" she whispered.

"I'm very sorry, Mrs. Henderson. I—"

Marie's mind whirled. Those were definitely footfalls on the stairs. She told herself it was probably one of her friends from the adjacent shops. She told herself it was broad daylight and she was perfectly safe. She told the woman on the other end of the phone something else.

"Listen," Marie breathed into the receiver. "I'm at my shop and I think someone is breaking in. I can't stay on the phone. Get the message to Lucas, please."

Marie let the phone drop and bolted for the door. She got there at the same moment he did. She had no reason to fear him. He had been a good customer. Relief flooded her as she smiled up at him. A relief that was short-lived.

"WHAT DOES THAT MEAN?" Lucas asked his broker.

"It means that Dr. Markum apparently didn't want anyone, including Uncle Sam, to know how he was hiding his money."

"Are you sure?"

She nodded. "I have a friend at the bank. He verified everything I suspected."

"When did he make the last transfer?"

"About an hour before his body was discovered."

"Thanks," Lucas said, offering his hand. At that instant, his pager sounded.

"Feel free to use the phone," his broker offered.

"Thanks." Lucas dialed the number to his office. "This is Dr. Henderson," he said to the unfamiliar female voice that answered.

"Your wife is in trouble."

"Who are you?"

"I'm Gretchen. I'm filling in for your secretary while she's on vacation. But listen, I got an urgent call from your wife."

Lucas listened impatiently as she told him about Marie's call. He didn't even thank her before he cut the connection. "Do you have a telephone book?" Lucas asked.

"Is everything okay?"

"No."

Marie wasn't listed, but the shop was. He tried the number but she didn't pick up. He tried to convince himself that the phone must have been damaged during the shooting. She was probably just hearing the wind and had been frightened. He didn't want to imagine any other scenario.

"I need another favor," Lucas said, and he grabbed a pen and began writing. "Call this number and ask for Lieutenant Peltier. Tell him I'm at this address and I need help *now*."

The few blocks to Heaven Scent felt more like a hundred. Lucas weaved through the tourists and vendors as he ran along the uneven sidewalk. His heart was in his throat by the time he got to the shop.

"Marie?" he called, plunging through a gap in the boards. "Marie!"

He prayed as he took the backstairs like hurdles. "Marie?"

The door was open. Her purse was on the floor. The bottle of antibiotics had fallen out. The sound of sirens grew closer. They were too late.

He was too late.

"What's the problem?" Peltier asked when he arrived a few minutes later.

Lucas grabbed him and dragged him back to the police car. "We need the address of a man named Rossner."

"First name?" Peltier asked.

"I don't know. I only know his wife's first name. Amanda."

Peltier lifted his radio and had an address in a matter of minutes. "Now what?"

"Take me there."

"Lucas," he cautioned. "I'm not a taxi. I need to know the problem before—"

"The man has my wife."

"Marie Delacroix?"

"Yes. He killed David."

"How do you know that? Last time we talked—"

"I'll tell you everything while we drive. We can't be too far behind them."

"Get in."

MARIE SAT BEHIND the wheel of the beige four-door with the rusted-out fenders that Lucas had described.

"I don't understand," she began in a calm voice. "I've never done anything to you."

"Shut up," he said, jabbing the gun into her ribs. "Take the next exit."

Marie complied, but in doing so she reopened her wound on the hairpin she had hastily tucked inside the bandage. She could feel the blood but no pain. With luck, she thought grimly, her death would be the same way.

"All I did was sell you some oil," Marie said. "Please, Mr. Rogers, I—"

"I told you to be quiet," he growled. "My name isn't Rogers, it's Rossner."

Rossner? The name was familiar. She racked her brain as she followed his instructions to the letter. It wasn't until she turned into a long, deserted driveway that she made the connection. *Rossner* was one of the names she had seen in David's files at Haven. Everything started to fall into place. This man, who had been coming into her shop since it opened, had to have been the one who'd tampered with her oil. But why?

"Stop here," he said when they neared the house. "Now get out. We're going around back."

Marie winced but didn't cry out as she purposefully coaxed blood from her hand. On the off chance that someone had seen her being led from the apartment at gunpoint, she wanted to provide them with every opportunity to find her.

"I have money," she tried.

He laughed derisively. "So do I."

They headed away from the house and passed a rusty oil tank. Rossner pushed her from behind and

Marie stumbled, catching herself before she actually fell. "You don't have to hurt me."

"It wasn't part of the plan until you got married and your husband started asking around. You were supposed to die in a car accident. It was supposed to be simple. I planned it out for months. Ever since you helped Markum try to make a fool of me."

"How did I do that?"

He snorted and shoved her in the direction of a stand of pine trees. "They were adulterers, and you helped them hide their deceptions. But you didn't fool me."

Marie suddenly realized where he was taking her. They were heading toward a small building set back a hundred yards or so in the woods, completely hidden from the main house. She tried to touch as many things as she could without alerting her captor.

Marie took a deep, sobbing breath. She didn't want to die in the woods like some mongrel. She had to think.

"Open the door," Rossner commanded, once they'd reached the shack.

She spun around and glared back at him. "If you're going to kill me, you won't get my help."

Rossner's smile was purely evil and his eyes hinted at madness. "I'm not going to shoot you."

"You're not?"

"It's a waste of ammunition," he said, and drew back the hand that held the gun.

A starburst of color exploded before Marie's eyes as the gun connected with the side of her head. Then there was nothing but blackness.

"I'LL KILL HIM with my bare hands!"

"Wait," Peltier ordered, grabbing Lucas's arm. "We can't rush the house, we might spook him."

"We can't even get close to the house without him seeing us," Lucas said. "There's nothing but open land on all sides."

"I've got to call this in," Peltier told him. "We'll get the hostage negotiators up here."

Lucas met the lieutenant's eyes and nodded. As soon as Peltier released his arm, he sprang from the car.

Weaving like some sort of star running back shagging tacklers, Lucas managed to reach the beige car without any apparent notice from inside the house. He crouched at the rear of the old car, trying to decide on his next move.

Slowly, his eyes glued to the front of the house, he worked his way around to the driver's side. As he did so, he glanced at the driver's door and noticed the slight reddish smear. Blood.

Panic quickly gave way to relief when he detected further drops on the gravel. "Way to go, Marie," he whispered as he followed the trail around the side of the house.

The drops stopped suddenly, and he felt the swell of panic return. At the same instant a bullet came whizzing over his head. He dove for the car, then rolled in the dirt until he lay beneath it.

Sirens blared as Peltier drove up the driveway, drawing fire from Rossner's gun. Lucas used the diversion to scramble from beneath the car and race over to the house. Kicking in the door, he stumbled inside.

Bullets were still flying outside. Lucas knew he couldn't get to Marie unless he had a weapon. If Rossner had one gun, statistics said he would have another.

Statistics held true. Lucas found a cabinet with a well-stocked gun rack in one of the rooms. After wrapping his arm in a towel from the bathroom, he broke the glass and yanked out the first gun he touched. It happened to be a rifle. An *unloaded* rifle.

Lucas's curse was muffled by the rapid exchange of gunfire outside. He started tearing the room apart, looking for bullets, anything that would allow him to get to Marie. He realized that the gunfire had stopped at the same time that he heard the footsteps in the hall. He breathed a sigh of relief and ran out of the den to thank Peltier.

"No." It was the only word Lucas could articulate when he found himself standing in the small hallway with the barrel of a large-caliber gun just inches from his chest.

Rossner smiled wildly before he raised the barrel so that it was pointed directly at Lucas's forehead. Then a single shot rang out.

EPILOGUE

MARIE WAS IN ONE of the cubicles in the emergency room, waiting to have her stitches replaced. She wished they would get on with it so she could find out if Peltier was really going to be okay.

"How are we doing?" an elderly doctor asked cheerily as he slipped through the curtain flanked by an equally chipper nurse. "It says here that you're married to one of the staff physicians. I guess that explains why you're getting the VIP treatment."

"I'm afraid I don't understand."

"I'm Dr. Collingsworth. I'm the head of plastic and reconstructive surgery."

"Oh." Marie blushed. "I didn't realize."

"Dr. Carl Lee called me himself."

"That was nice," Marie commented. She turned away when he started to remove her bandage. "You didn't happen to hear how Officer Peltier is doing?"

"Who?"

"That's the officer they brought in with the gunshot wound," the attending nurse offered.

"If it will put Mrs. Henderson at ease, why don't you see if you can get her a status."

The nurse disappeared through the curtain. "I've got good news and bad news," Dr. Collingsworth said.

"Nothing you could say to me could be any worse than what I've gone through today," Marie assured him.

"The good news is that I'm confident this wound will heal completely. Even with the additional damage."

"What's the bad news?"

"There's a lot of swelling, so we're going to have to cut your wedding ring off."

Marie just nodded. It would come off in a matter of hours, anyway. Shelby had already come by and promised her that she'd have Marie completely exonerated before her head hit the pillow.

"There's nothing to worry about," the nurse announced. "Officer Peltier is already out of surgery. The bullet didn't do anything more serious than fracture his collarbone."

"That's good news." Marie sighed. "Is Lucas still with him?"

The nurse looked shocked. "He was here a little while ago. I just assumed he had spoken to you before he left."

"He left?" Marie repeated.

"About a half hour ago. I don't think he was feeling very well."

Marie felt a pinch, then Dr. Collingsworth reached around and handed her the two halves of her ring. It seemed almost symbolic in a macabre sort of way. Marie felt tears sting her eyes as she jingled the pieces of the ring in her palm.

"I'll put that in a bag for you," the nurse offered. She took the pieces and examined them. "I'm sure a jeweler can repair this. Oh, but maybe not the inscription.''

''Inscription?''

''Yes. Unless you change the one word to *real*. But that sounds kind of funny.''

''Can I see?'' Marie asked over the lump in her throat.

The nurse held the ring up so that the carefully inscribed words were legible. ''I really do love you,'' she read. Desiree's words returned to her. ''When the ring comes off...''

''Excuse me?'' the nurse said.

Marie smiled. ''Something a friend told me. Can we hurry? I've got an appointment with another doctor.''

''YOU DON'T LOOK SO GOOD,'' Lucas said when he opened the door.

He didn't invite her in.

''I don't know. I think I'm doing pretty well for a woman who's been kidnapped, beaten, shot at, locked in a shed with a skeleton and forced to pick the lock to free herself. And then offered assistance to a policeman who'd been shot by a madman. Did I forget anything?''

''You saved my life.''

''I did,'' Marie agreed. ''But you were going to do the same for me.''

''Peltier's going to be fine,'' he said with a smile that didn't reach his eyes. ''If you hadn't taken his gun and come after Rossner, he would have killed me.''

"I know," Marie said, searching his pained expression.

"It was pretty smart of you to leave that trail of blood."

"I know."

"I guess I'm glad you're so adept at picking locks. I think Rossner had planned to leave you to starve slowly in that shed."

"I know."

"They think those were his wife's remains in the shed. Amanda was David's mistress."

"I know."

"David was planning on taking her away. They must have known that Rossner was dangerous and violent and would probably search for them unless they left the country. My broker found out David had been shipping his money offshore for a while. Rossner must have known about it all along. By the way, he's a chemist," Lucas said with a small laugh. "That's how he knew what to do to poison David. They told me he was going to survive the shooting."

"I know."

"So I guess that about wraps everything up. Except... Who is the red-haired woman? It wasn't Amanda Rossner—she was a brunette."

Marie sighed. "I guess we'll never know."

"What did Dr. Collingsworth say about your hand?"

Marie saw her opening and took it. "He had good news and bad news."

Lucas's response was just what she had hoped for. He quickly ushered her into the condo. Marie had to step over two opened suitcases. "Going some-where?"

"Just a vacation. What's the bad news?"

Marie tugged her arm free. "You were going to skip out and not tell me?"

Lucas raked his fingers through his hair. "I just needed some time," he said. "I haven't felt as pow-erless and useless as I did today since I lost my par-ents."

Marie reached up with the intention of touching his face. Lucas grabbed her wrist.

"Let's not make this harder than it has to be."

"Okay." She dropped her hand and turned to leave. "I just came by to tell you one thing."

"What?"

"I really do love you." Marie didn't even take the next step before she was lifted into his strong arms and kissed hard on the mouth.

"Give me the bad news," he said, gingerly kissing the dark bruise where Rossner had hit her. "Whatever it is, I can fix it."

She laughed. "That's arrogant. Now, put me down."

"Nope," he said as he carried her toward the bed-room. "What's the bad news?"

"They had to cut my wedding band off."

Lucas threw his head back and laughed. "Is that all? That's probably for the best, anyway. We can go together and pick out a new one for you."

"I have the pieces, and I'm sure you went to a lot of trouble to get that one—"

Marie was silenced when he lowered her to the bed and kissed her again. This was a different kind of kiss.

The passion was tempered by what she now knew was love. Her heart swelled and she gloried in the sheer joy of knowing she was loved.

They didn't talk again until much, much later. And only then because the telephone rang.

"Yes, she is." Lucas covered the telephone and said, "It's Shelby."

Marie took the phone. "Hi. Do you have lots of great news for me?"

"You'll be the lead story on the eleven o'clock news. All charges have been dropped—you're a free woman now!"

"Thanks, Shelby, I guess you can send me a bill." She handed Lucas the phone.

No sooner had Lucas replaced the receiver than it rang again. "Hello, Beau. No, you may not speak to her right now. She's fine. Tell your entire family that she's in good hands and she'll talk to you in a few days."

Lucas! she mouthed.

"Goodbye, Beau. And pass the word—Marie is not taking calls for a while. Bye."

Marie felt warm. "I can't believe you told my brother that I'm not available. He's probably howling because he will know exactly what we're doing."

"If you have the guts to waltz in here and tell me that you love me, you can handle a little ribbing from big brother."

"It didn't take guts," she said, curling up in his arms.

"I couldn't have done it."

"But your way was so much better."

"I'm glad you finally realized that I was doing my best to show you how I felt."

Marie's hand stilled. "What?"

"Once I realized that you had mistaken my teasing for condescension, I decided to change my ways. I wanted you to see that even though I'm pretty grounded in science, I'm willing to learn. We don't have to think with one mind to love each other."

"What…what about my wedding ring?"

"It doesn't matter, Marie. I found it in a jewelry store in the Quarter for half price. The original purchaser never picked it up."

"You didn't custom order this ring?"

He frowned. "No. As a matter of fact, I forgot all about a ring until I was on my way to the courthouse. I guessed at your ring size and bought the first one the jeweler had that would fit you. I'll replace it with whatever your heart desires."

Marie started laughing and couldn't stop for the longest time.

"Want to tell me what's so funny?"

"Nope."

Looping her arms around his neck, she lowered his head to hers and gave him a long, lingering kiss.

"Some secrets," she said, "are meant for keeping."

DELTA JUSTICE

continues with

EVERY KID NEEDS A HERO

by Candace Shuler

Jacqueline Delacroix's world was horses. She'd long ago given up any dreams of being a traditional wife and mother. Matt Taggart's world was his veterinary practice and his two young children. He couldn't imagine that "The Fabulous Jax" would ever look his way. But she couldn't resist him, and suddenly romance at Riverwood changed both their worlds.

Available in January

Here's a preview!

EVERY KID NEEDS
A HERO

"THAT WAS SOME KISS," Matt said gruffly, in a voice that sounded as if it came from somebody else.

"Mmm," Jax agreed, and nuzzled his cheek, trying to recapture his mouth with hers. "More."

He shifted his hands to her shoulders and held her away a little, waiting until she opened her eyes to look at him before he tried to explain.

"Matt?" she said, blinking in confusion.

"I don't have anything with me. Protection," he said when she continued to stare up at him with a bewildered look in her eyes. "I'm sorry. I shouldn't have let it go this far. I shouldn't have even started it, I guess. It's just..." His one-sided smile was wry and self-mocking. "I've been wanting to kiss you for weeks."

"Weeks?"

"Months, really," he admitted. "I've been wanting to kiss you for months. Ever since you came back to Bayou Beltane, in fact."

Jax was charmed. And flattered. And vaguely disappointed that their kisses wouldn't lead to more. "You never even gave me a hint."

"Because I didn't want you to know. I thought the feeling would go away and—" He broke off, shaking his head. "No, that's not true. I didn't say anything because I knew it would happen just this way. I knew if I kissed you, I'd go crazy." He touched his forehead to hers. "You pack quite a punch, Miz Delacroix," he drawled, deliberately exaggerating his Louisiana accent to lighten the mood.

"I do?" she said, delighted. No one had ever said anything like that to her before. "Really?"

"You do," he affirmed, wondering why she seemed so surprised.

"So do you," Jax whispered. "Pack quite a punch, I mean," she added, and offered her lips.

He groaned, and took them.

The kiss was hot and sweet and lasted long enough to have both of them breathing hard when it was over.

"No more," he said, dragging his mouth from hers. "Please. I'll go stark, raving insane if we do that again. And being obliged to get married isn't the best way to start a relationship."

"No, I don't guess it would be."

He reached out and touched her cheek, disturbed by the look on her face. Her expression was strangely distraught. "It's for both our sakes, sweetheart. I hope you realize that."

"Yes, of course," Jax said, wondering if she should just go ahead and tell him he didn't have to worry about her getting pregnant. But what did it matter, really? They weren't going to have sex. At least, not tonight. And when they did—if they did—he would be using protection. She'd never have to admit to her defects. "The last thing I'd want is an unplanned pregnancy," she said firmly.

He stroked his finger down her cheek. "Next

time," he murmured, "I'll be prepared. And, Jax—" he put his finger under her chin, turning her face up to his "—there *will* be a next time."

"You think so?" she said archly, trying to pretend a coolness she didn't feel.

"I know so. I haven't come this far to be scared off now." He pressed a soft kiss on her lips, then let her go. "Come on," he said, standing up and holding out his hand. "I'll walk you to your door—" he sent her a sideways glance, rife with anticipation and undisguised desire "—then you can kiss me good-night and I'll try to cop a feel."

HARLEQUIN SUPERROMANCE®

...there's more to the story!

Superromance. A *big* satisfying read about unforgettable characters. Each month we offer *four* very different stories that range from family drama to adventure and mystery, from highly emotional stories to romantic comedies—and much more! Stories about people you'll believe in and care about. Stories too compelling to put down....

Our authors are among today's *best* romance writers. You'll find familiar names and talented newcomers. Many of them are award winners—and you'll see why!

If you want the biggest and best in romance fiction, you'll get it from Superromance!

Available wherever Harlequin books are sold.

Look us up on-line at: http://www.romance.net

HS-GEN

HARLEQUIN PRESENTS®

HARLEQUIN PRESENTS
men you won't be able to resist
falling in love with...

HARLEQUIN PRESENTS
women who have feelings
just like your own...

HARLEQUIN PRESENTS
powerful passion in
exotic international settings...

HARLEQUIN PRESENTS
intense, dramatic stories that will keep you
turning to the very last page...

HARLEQUIN PRESENTS
The world's bestselling romance series!

PRES-G

HARLEQUIN®

AMERICAN ◆ ROMANCE®

LOOK FOR OUR FOUR FABULOUS MEN!

Each month some of today's bestselling authors bring
four new fabulous men to Harlequin American Romance.
Whether they're rebel ranchers, millionaire power brokers
or sexy single dads, they're all gallant princes—and
they're all ready to sweep you into lighthearted fantasies
and contemporary fairy tales where anything is possible
and where all your dreams come true!

You don't even have to make a wish...
Harlequin American Romance will grant your every desire!

Look for Harlequin American Romance
wherever Harlequin books are sold!

HAR-GEN

Harlequin® Historical

From rugged lawmen and
valiant knights to defiant heiresses
and spirited frontierswomen,
Harlequin Historicals will
capture your imagination with
their dramatic scope, passion
and adventure.

Harlequin Historicals...
they're too good to miss!

HHGENR

Harlequin Romance®

Delightful

Affectionate

Romantic

Emotional

Tender

Original

Daring

Riveting

Enchanting

Adventurous

Moving

Harlequin Romance—the
series that has it all!

HROM-G